AF390860

JOSIANE FORTIN

New Witch in Town

Contents

Prologue 1
Chapter 1 2
Chapter 2 12
Chapter 3 21
Chapter 4 41
Chapter 5 60
Chapter 6 77
Chapter 7 93
Chapter 8 130
Chapter 9 148
Chapter 10 164
About the Author 169

Prologue

My name is Emily.

To my dismay, my life had been quite ordinary until the day a significant event disturbed my routine, upending my peaceful and—let's admit it—tedious life. I considered it the chance of a lifetime.

Flash back to how the arrival of a new girl changed my monotonous life as a teenager in a quiet town. Or, in other words, how I became a witch's apprentice.

Chapter 1

The timid late-summer sun tickled my face. Although I had drawn the curtains before bed, the rays were making their way through the hole my cat had savagely created the week before. Clenching my eyelids tightly, hoping to get back to sleep, I rolled over and pulled the duvet over my head. It was no use. Already I was thinking about what I was going to wear to school this morning. I mentally reviewed the clothes in my wardrobe. My black skirt with my new red top? No. I should save that outfit for Friday because I had an oral presentation to make, and I wanted to look my best in front of the Spanish class. Especially since Christian would be in the audience.

My cigarette jeans and blue blouse? Yes. Simple and comfortable. The perfect outfit for a Monday morning.

I groaned and forced myself to sit up. The school year at Frankville High, a boring school in a boring rural Canadian town, had only started a week earlier, and I was already having trouble getting out of bed.

I liked these moments when I was alone, before the entire house woke up. I'd barely had the thought when my cat, Kenzo—more commonly known as Ken—pushed open the door and jumped onto my bed to build his nest among the messy sheets. Once comfortably installed, he licked his paws while observing me.

Although he was an ordinary alley cat adopted from the pound when he was just a baby, Ken acted like he was a king in his kingdom. He had a gray coat with a white stripe running from the tip of his muzzle to the top of his head. I loved him very much. I sat on my bed and scratched the top of his head, and he purred more and more.

Now fully awake, I pushed back the sheets gently so as not to disturb Ken. As soon as I got up, I used a flat iron on my hair, a routine I did every morning. The ritual was necessary because my brown hair was thick and frizzy. I had to discipline my mane every day. Otherwise, my appearance would suffer irreparably. No way would I show up at school with a lion's mane.

I hopped into my skinny jeans and buttoned my blue cotton blouse then slipped my favorite earrings into my earlobes, gold rings that my grandmother had given me on a girls' shopping trip last month. I took my tube of black mascara and applied two coats to my long, full lashes. With my hair slicked back and falling loosely over my shoulders, I took one last look in the mirror before leaving my room for breakfast.

My room was in the basement my parents had built. I walked through the playroom and up the stairs with sleepy steps. My little sister, Lillian, was already running around the house. It amazed me how much energy she displayed so early in the morning. Even though she was ten years old, Lillian still liked to play with her dolls. Sometimes she wanted to be like the grown-ups, but she was still a child.

As for me, I had stopped playing with dolls a long time ago. At sixteen, I had much more important things to worry about.

Like my history test that afternoon. And my Spanish oral presentation on Friday. I wasn't a perfectionist, but I liked to do well in school, and I had to put in the effort to get good grades. I had spent an afternoon this weekend revising my history notes, and I was ready. Still, I felt a few butterflies in my stomach at the thought of what lay ahead.

I burst into the kitchen. My sister came by to give me a quick hug and continued on her way.

My father was sitting at the lunch counter, checking his email while gulping his cereal. My mother was racing to empty the dishwasher.

"Hello, everyone!"

I grabbed my favorite bowl from the cupboard. It was an old plastic bowl with faded drawings of Pocahontas on the sides. It had been through thousands of cycles in the dishwasher and was just the right size. Despite its faded appearance, cereal always tasted better in it.

That was what I ate every morning. It did not bore me since I ate all kinds—wheat, oat, honey, maple, sliced, squares. I poured some cereal into my bowl and dug in. Today, my spoon held the four-grain cereal.

I deliberately ignored the surrounding cacophony, the easiest way to make my existence more tolerable. My mother was desperately trying to get my sister on track. Lillian was still in her pajamas, even though it was late. She kept saying that she didn't want breakfast, that she wasn't hungry. My father, having swallowed his cereal, was frantically preparing everyone's lunches. Every morning, he would grumble that he should get into the habit of making the lunches the night before, but like he did every morning, he rushed to finish in time.

After polishing off my cereal, I walked around my father to put my bowl and spoon in the dishwasher. Then I went to the bathroom to brush my teeth, came back downstairs and grabbed my lunch box that my dad had just put on the counter. I threw my backpack over my shoulder and walked out the door, shouting a quick goodbye to everyone. As the door closed behind me, I took a deep breath. Finally, some peace.

There was a pleasant breeze that morning as I walked. Although school wasn't too far from my house, the walk gave me a chance to think. Christian was often at the center of my thoughts. It had been almost a year since he had moved to Frankville. The first moment I'd seen him, my heart had skipped a beat. Unfortunately, the attraction traveled only one way, and I was not the only one to fall for his charm—all my friends had noticed him too. He had dark hair and intriguing blue eyes. How many times had I seen his face in my dreams? It was almost an obsession.

Providentially, he was in my Spanish class. For once, luck was on my side. I had spoken to him only a few times, but since I turned red as a tomato when I did, I preferred to avoid it.

He'd been dating Maria for a month. I was getting angry just thinking about it. Maria, the most beautiful girl in school, had obviously gotten her hooks into him. Of South American origin, she had a dreamy tan complexion, long jet-black hair, and beautiful big brown eyes. She looked like a model. Of course, Christian would fall for her rather than me—a skinny, pale teenager with an unruly mane.

I kicked a pebble that was unfortunate enough to be on the sidewalk. The pebble didn't deserve it, but it was the only outlet for my anger.

I was still grumbling when I arrived at school. I definitely had to move on. This thing with Christian was eating away at me unnecessarily. He seemed so in love with Maria that I had no chance of changing his mind. Especially since I had always been invisible to him.

I walked through the school doors to meet my friends at our table in the common area. The tables were generally for seniors. It was an unwritten code. If the younger students dared to sit at one of the tables, the older students bullied them until they left. However, we had claimed the table next to the toilet that nobody wanted. Although the area sometimes smelled bad, we wouldn't give up our table for anything. As juniors, we felt important and special at that table, admitted by default by the older students.

Caroline and Morgan were already there. Caroline was chewing her cinnamon gum as usual. I thought she must have a sore jaw both from the chewing and her constant brooding. Morgan was laughing, and I figured out Caroline was telling her about her family weekend at the cottage. I took a seat next to them and listened with a distracted ear. The other members of the group arrived at brief intervals. Vanessa, a slender blonde who always wore jeans and sneakers. Jocelyn, nicknamed Joe, who always followed the latest diet. And Ashley, who had short hair and always had a smile on her face. She was the sportiest of the six of us.

Since the beginning of the school year, I had been more or less taking part in the conversations. We had been friends for so long that I was getting bored with the routine—the predictable comments, the endless conversations about the latest accessories, the jokes that we had laughed at dozens of times before. I felt like I was inexorably drifting away from my friends. Our priorities and interests were unfortunately no longer the same. I felt more and more different. Alone in the crowd.

Distracted, I didn't really listen to the insipid babble from my friends. From the corner of my eye, I watched Christian and Maria, who seemed to get along well. I wanted to see them bicker, but nothing seemed to disturb their union. Yet hope still burned inside me, despite all the reasoning and logic I used to try to extinguish it.

The hubbub in the common area grew louder as more buses arrived with their streams of students. The bell announcing the start of classes rang. Everyone got up to retrieve their books from their cubicles and headed to their first classes. I slipped away with relief. I had no desire to hear more about the wooden bracelets worn by Elvira Ramirez at the premiere of her latest film, *Conquest on the Beach*.

With my books in my arms, I headed to my classroom. My day began with an English class. What a bore. For the past five years, the teachers had been harping on the same old stuff about past participles. Were we all so stupid that we couldn't move on? Apparently, some of us had to be told the same thing repeatedly in order to keep up.

Once again, I listened with a distracted ear. To pass the time, I drew psychedelic patterns in my diary. I carefully filled in the dozens of little squares that made up an original drawing. I had several colored pens I used for my work.

I'd created an array of drawings in my planner, many of which cleverly camouflaged the name Christian among the intricate lines. I didn't want to shout my obsession with his blue eyes from the rooftops. Anyway, there was little chance of anyone deciphering my drawings. I didn't like to show my creations. They were too personal.

In the afternoon, it was time for my history exam. A few questions took me by surprise, but overall I thought I did pretty well since I finished a few minutes before the bell. My brain felt drained after so much concentration. Fortunately, it was the last class of the day. I handed my copy of the test to the teacher. He nodded in acknowledgement, and I gave him a forced smile. Some students were still bent over their papers, eagerly scribbling down their answers before the teacher told them to put down their pencils.

I left the room, relieved that one thing was settled. Now I could focus on the oral presentation for my Spanish class that was coming up on Friday. The topic was "The Family," which would allow students to use our basic vocabulary. I still didn't know exactly what I was going to say. It was a great opportunity to get Christian's attention. I wanted him to notice me and to find me interesting, beautiful, and funny. Well, I could dream.

Before leaving school, I collected my things from my locker. Unfortunately, I had some homework to do for the next day, including a math assignment. I slammed the door to my locker with a confident movement, secured the lock, and headed out. Lost in my thoughts, I hardly noticed the route. I walked mechanically, reciting in my head Spanish phrases that I could use for my presentation.

When I entered the house, I was alone. The cat greeted me, rubbing himself gracefully between my legs. My father was at the office while my mother took Lillian to her dance class after work. I liked these moments of solitude and used the quiet time to complete my homework. I would have the rest of the evening to entertain myself.

I sat down at the kitchen table. I was having a little difficulty concentrating on my work that night. My routine was becoming increasingly boring. My friends liked me less and less, and I understood them too well. I hardly took part in their conversations anymore because I was sick of pretending to be interested in their inane chatter. It was no longer of any interest to me, as I aimed to discuss the meaning of life, current events, the future, and not gossip about the neighbors. I regretted that I couldn't relate to them anymore. To be honest, I was changing, and they were staying true to themselves.

Besides, I felt excluded. But what other group could I fit into? As I mentally reviewed the different groups, I realized I was different from all the students. I no longer belonged at this school. I needed new friends, but that was easier said than done. In the meantime, I resolved to try harder not to be pushed out of my group because I had no intention of being elected loser-with-no-friends.

I hurriedly finished my homework and grabbed a green apple from the fridge. My mom worked hard to make sure we always had healthy snacks on hand. I took a juicy bite out of the fruit and curled up on the couch to watch my favorite TV show before dinner. *The Simpsons.*

My mother and sister soon arrived, with my father following closely behind. The daily hustle and bustle of the house began again. I preferred to stay away from the commotion. I usually set the table and then hid in my room until my dad called me to eat. As soon as we cleared the table after dinner, I went back to the basement to listen to music, study, read, or write in my journal.

My mother sometimes looked at me disapprovingly, but she respected my lifestyle. As I overheard her say while she was talking to her sister on the phone, I was apparently going through my *teenager phase.* I didn't see how seeking silence in such a busy house was weird. I had no desire to talk to her about it. It didn't matter anyway.

The next day, I was sitting at our table with my friends—as bored as ever—when a wave of excitement spread through the common area. The atmosphere changed dramatically, causing my arms to break out in goose bumps. Something unusual was definitely happening.

Like my friends, ready to do anything to avoid missing out on juicy gossip, I turned my head in all directions, looking for the source of this activity.

I saw her in the doorway of the main entrance.

A new student. In such a small town, we rarely had new students at our school, let alone a student who started a week late. Why hadn't she started at the same time as all of us? Although her late arrival was a surprise, it wasn't the strangest thing about her.

Her appearance stood out in this sea of conformity. This girl had bright-red hair that appeared almost iridescent when she turned her head. Her linen clothes made her look like a hippie ready to go to war, an unusual combination. Her piercing green eyes defied the crowd of curious onlookers. I would have blushed from head to toe if I had been in such a situation. Not her. She didn't even look down.

My friends whispered excitedly, as did all the other students. They were commenting on the newcomer's unusual clothing. More judgments based on superficial criteria. Exasperated by their behavior, I stopped listening.

Instead, I focused all my attention on the new girl. She fascinated me. Her green eyes met mine briefly. Intimidated, I turned away immediately, blushing. I pretended to be immersed in the conversation going on at my table. Fortunately, the bell rang soon afterward. I glanced at the door. The new girl had disappeared.

Chapter 2

As I walked out of math, my first class of the day, I headed to my locker to put my books in as usual. I slammed the gray metal door shut. It startled me to see the new girl leaning against the opposite wall, looking at me as she bit into a red apple. She stood on one foot, the other raised behind her. I put my hand over my still-racing heart. What was she waiting for, and why was she watching me?

She approached me with feline steps, swallowed her mouthful of apple, and said casually, "Hi, there."

I wasn't sure how to react. She intrigued me and frightened me at the same time. I glanced around briefly to make sure she was talking to me. She took another bite of apple and chewed, looking cheerful. I knew we were the center of attention in the hallway. Indeed, the other students were watching us discreetly—or was that just my impression? Pulling myself together, I knew I had to greet her in return, if only out of politeness. Unsure of myself, I gave her a casual "hi."

She smiled at me with her white, aligned teeth. I felt like I had passed her test. Her confidence intimidated me, but I calmed my anxiety by telling myself that she wouldn't suddenly start insulting or hitting me—well, I hoped she wouldn't. She finished her apple and threw the core into the trash. She wiped her hand on her jeans and introduced herself. "I'm Brianna. I just moved here."

She went on to explain that her parents had sent her to stay with her aunt because they were going on a yearlong pilgrimage to Asia. Such a radical change in her life didn't seem to sadden her in the least.

In a few minutes, she gave me a glimpse into her world. We chatted with the utmost naturalness. It was as if we had known each other forever. I drank in her words. I found her fascinating. She had traveled to many parts of the world.

"My parents like to go on adventures, and I used to accompany them everywhere. Except this time, I wanted to experience what it's like to have a normal and stable life," she said.

She definitely overestimated the happiness that an ordinary life like mine could bring her.

The time went by so fast that the bell signaling the end of the break surprised me. I hadn't even noticed that we had been standing in the hallway talking the whole time. I had discovered that I had something in common with Brianna, and she inspired me. She was a breath of fresh air in this school, just when I was suffocating.

Brianna walked away, and I collected my books for the next period. As I walked to my physics class, I could feel the inquisitive looks from the other students. Had my conversation with Brianna already made it around the school?

At lunchtime, I took my place at our usual spot in the cafeteria. We had a table in the back of the room, near the canteen cash register. I had barely put my tray down when the girls started bombarding me with questions. They wanted to know all about my discussion with Brianna. I sensed instinctively that they loathed her presence at our school. She was too different, and it troubled them. It did not surprise me in the least. Ignorant people are always afraid of people who are not like them. I rolled my eyes.

The girls were chattering excitedly and commenting on every new piece of information they got from me. Suddenly, I felt a thick uneasiness spread around the table and envelop us. Without even seeing her, I felt Brianna heading straight for us.

The questions suddenly stopped raining down on me, and the girls tried their best to keep calm. Morgan launched into another subject in order to animate the girls at the table, but she lacked conviction. She wanted to hide from Brianna the fact that a few seconds earlier, we'd been talking about her behind her back.

Brianna put her tray down in front of me. The new girl was imposing herself without a trace of embarrassment into our group. I admired her nerve.

"Can I sit here?" she asked, smiling at the group.

She took her seat without waiting for an answer. Apparently, she didn't care what the others thought of her.

The girls probably would have preferred to see her vanish from the face of the earth rather than have her around. They weren't chatting with their usual gusto. Vanessa, who was on Brianna's right, was squirming nervously in her chair. She was munching her meal without appetite. Brianna ignored her. Joe was pecking at her plate instead of devouring her food as she usually did.

Brianna took up the conversation with me where we had left off at the break, with disconcerting simplicity. How I wished I had her confidence.

Shortly before the bell was about to ring, Brianna walked

away with her tray after saying goodbye. As if revived by her departure, my friends started chatting. Her incursion had scandalized them.

"Wait, who does she think she is? Nobody invited her!" Vanessa's face was red with anger. If she got any angrier, she would spit on the floor in contempt, like a grumpy old woman. *What a charade!* I rolled my eyes in exasperation.

"Calm down," Morgan said. "She doesn't know anyone here. We could at least give her a chance."

Finally, some common sense. *Bravo, Morgan!*

"I'd like to agree with you, but that girl gives me the creeps," Caroline said, chewing her cinnamon gum. "Besides"—she added, leaning toward us—"did you see everyone watching us? We can't accept just anyone in our group." She spoke her last words loudly and sat up straight. "Our reputation is on the line."

She reinforced her point by banging her fist on the table.

The girls nodded in unison. They had formed a pact.

I didn't even have time to speak. I didn't know what to say anyway. They were right about Brianna being strange. Her attire made her different—a little too different for a conservative place like Frankville.

The girls wanted to exclude her from the group. But her arrival had disrupted my sorry routine. I felt as if my life brightened up in her presence. She gave me wings, the desire to go for it and make all my dreams come true. She gave me a glimpse of a wonderful life outside this conformist city.

Talking with her had been stimulating. Brianna had visited several countries, experienced different cultures, and was open to the world and intelligent thought, whereas our group had traveled little outside Quebec. The record distance belonged to Ashley, who had been lucky enough to see New York, thanks to her selection to play in a volleyball tournament. I had never even set foot outside the region, except on a school trip to Ottawa. But Brianna…

I was going to have to choose between my friendship with Brianna and my relationship with my other friends. But, in my brief life, such a strong, instant connection to somebody was new to me.

The next day, Brianna came to sit across from me in the cafeteria once again. This was her second day at school, and it relieved me to see that her novelty was already wearing off. The students no longer systematically turned around as she passed. She would soon become part of the scenery. I was happy for her. It must have been hard to bear all those curious looks.

During the meal, we discovered we had a lot in common despite our different backgrounds. She liked cats. She had ambition, a rare thing in this small town, and she was thinking big. Her head was bubbling with a lot of projects she wanted to tackle. And to think that just a few days ago, I was dreaming of having a friend like her in my life.

She and I had a great time laughing and learning about each other. My friends gossiped among themselves and didn't join in. Caroline gave me a few angry glances to let me know of her disapproval, but I was too happy to pay much attention to her. Brianna ignored Caroline and the others. Unfortunately, Brianna had to leave before lunch break was over to see her history teacher. "An exam to review," she told me. "Quite standard when you move in the middle of the school year."

So Brianna stood up and pushed back her thick, red hair.

"Bye!" she said as she walked away, exuding a disarming

confidence.

She did not know what was going on behind her back. Neither did I.

Enthusiastically, I turned to the girls. "She's great, isn't she?"

From the looks on their faces, I knew things were going to get ugly. I sensed the girls didn't have the same opinion as me. Why had I been stupid enough to think that Brianna would change their minds about her?

As soon as Brianna was far enough away from our table not to overhear, Morgan whispered, "Look, we have to get rid of her."

To my dismay, all the girls nodded. I shook my head in annoyance. They had been plotting behind my back all along. I felt betrayed. Suspecting that I was going to protest, Morgan turned to me. Apparently, she was the spokesperson for the group.

"Emily, we've discussed this, and we all agree that we should exclude her from the group. And since she's sitting with us because of you, you have to tell her. Basic logic. Tell her we don't want her."

"Right!" Joe said.

"The sooner the better," Morgan said.

The other girls regarded me, shaking their heads. Only Caroline looked down. She seemed uncomfortable with the turn of events. She gave me hope, and I tried a last plea.

"She is new and will eat alone without our friendship," I said. "She has no one else. Let her adjust to her new life, and I'm sure you'll adopt her. She's a sweetheart."

The girls avoided my gaze and shook their heads. Clearly, I was preaching to a choir that had already made up their minds.

"That's not our problem. We don't want her. You get rid of

her, period," Morgan said, crossing her arms over her chest.

"You choose. It's her or us," Joe said.

Their selfishness disgusted me, but the girls had backed me into a corner. I didn't want to be kicked out of the group. I wasn't ready to say goodbye to my standing at this school. On the other hand, I hated the thought of pushing Brianna away. I wasn't okay with doing the dirty work. She was going to be on her own, and I could imagine how that would feel. I had never had to deal with a move before. I had known my friends since kindergarten. Being the new girl must be lonely, and I sympathized with her situation. Eating alone in the cafeteria—*what a shame!* Not knowing where to go during breaks—*what an embarrassment!* More importantly, I liked Brianna.

Now all the eyes of my friends were on me. Obviously, the girls were waiting for my answer. Stammering, I agreed to tell Brianna to leave us alone. My friends expected nothing less from me. Satisfied, they stood in unison and picked up their trays. Staying behind, I rested my head in my hands. I was a little shocked at myself for agreeing to commit such a cruel act. I had buckled under pressure like a twig under the massive foot of a mammoth.

Finally, I got up to return my tray. The cafeteria was almost empty now. The bell announcing the imminent start of my next class rang. I dragged my feet to my locker. I wasn't looking forward to this little chat with Brianna.

For the first time in my life, my history class went a little too fast for my liking. I had resolved to deal with the Brianna problem as soon as possible, like at the afternoon break. I was the type of person who would abruptly remove a bandage, preferring a quick and intense pain to a sustained pain over a longer period.

I had no trouble spotting Brianna. She appeared behind my locker door, as if by magic. She seemed to have already made a habit of it. I realized I did not know where her locker could be. Sadly, I realized it didn't matter anymore.

I led her to the cafeteria. Although most of the tables had been put away after lunch, a few tables remained for those who wanted to sit. The rest were folded up and leaning against the wall. The place was not very busy during the breaks, so we were going to have privacy.

She seemed delighted that I wanted to talk to her. After all, I was her first and only friend in Frankville. I swallowed hard. What I was about to say would not amuse her. Not at all.

"Brianna, listen," I said, clearing my throat. "I have nothing against you personally."

A questioning look filled her green eyes. She did not know what I was getting at. I wrung my hands nervously on the table.

"But the girls don't like to eat with you," I said. Gathering my courage, I confessed, "In fact, they would like you to leave them alone."

"But you, Emily? Don't you want us to be friends? I thought we were getting along." Her eyes were misty with tears.

"Uh, actually…" I hesitated. I felt I had to think hard so as not to put my foot in it. The easiest way to get out of the conversation as quickly as possible was to pretend that I agreed with my friends.

"Yes, I agree with them," I said, trying to put a little more conviction into my words.

Brianna was crying now. Big, silent tears were rolling down her cheeks. But I had to deliver the final blow—the killing blow—to leave no doubt in her mind. The last thing I wanted was to have to relive this painful conversation.

"I don't think we can be friends anymore. I wish you'd stop coming to talk to me."

I could hardly have been clearer—it was a complete rejection. Defeated, Brianna stood up hurriedly and almost ran out of the cafeteria. She was crying her eyes out. I could feel my eyes watering, too, as I felt sorry for her. I felt guilty for not having stronger convictions. Hopefully, she could find her place at our school. But it wouldn't be with us.

I felt so depressed. With hunched shoulders, I made my way to the bathroom with difficulty. I locked myself in a stall for the rest of the break and swallowed my tears. What I had done shamed me. All I could do was forget about it and move on. We'd settled the matter. It was better to tell her right away and give her a chance to meet other people, right? I tried to convince myself of that.

Chapter 3

I only had two days left to prepare my presentation for the Spanish class on Friday. Brianna was avoiding me and I was avoiding her, but when I bumped into her, I could tell she was mad at me for leaving her out. She glared at me. I looked down, feeling my face turn red with shame.

On the other hand, my friends were relieved. They had quickly put the overwhelming Brianna story behind them. Their babbling was back to normal. They didn't have Brianna's tears on their consciences like I did. At least I had regained a few shreds of esteem in their eyes, although I definitely continued to lose my place with them these days. My heart was heavy.

Focusing on a school project was exactly what I needed to take my mind off things.

On Thursday evening, I considered several alternatives for the next day's outfit. Finally, the best option turned out to be the first one, the one I had thought of on Monday morning lying in bed—my black skirt with my new red patterned top. So on Friday morning when I woke up, my clothes were ready, where I'd wisely lined them up on the back of my chair.

I applied a little makeup. Nothing too flashy. I wasn't used to wearing much, and I didn't want to draw too much attention to myself either. Other people's eyes on me were unsettling. I took the time to pull some of my hair back. Inspecting myself from all angles in my mirror, I thought I was almost pretty. I winked at myself and grabbed my bag.

I arrived at our table a short time later and found the girls in conversation, even more noisy and cheerful than usual. What were they talking about? Some new gossip? Curious, I approached them, and they did not notice me until I was almost to the table.

"…and he took my number, so we're supposed to meet on Sat—" Ashley suddenly went silent when she saw me approaching.

"What's this about?" I asked. "Did you meet someone? Where did you meet someone?"

Ashley's face took on different shades of pink and red. I felt uneasy. I knew the girls were hiding something from me.

"Oh yeah," Ashley said. "It's just… yesterday I went out with my brother and his friends. We went to the Big Box."

"Did you get in?"

"Um, yes. We had fake IDs."

The bell rang, and I noticed how Caroline relaxed. In fact, all the girls looked relieved to be leaving for class, which confirmed that they weren't telling me the truth. They scurried away.

During third period, when I arrived at the Spanish class for my presentation, I inevitably blushed as soon as I opened my mouth. My blood was really playing tricks on me. As I felt the heat rising in my cheeks, I blushed even more.

The most painful part was feeling Christian's eyes on me. Did he think I was ridiculous, standing in front of the class with my face flushed?

Okay. Take a deep breath.

I went for it. I was well prepared and had learned my lines carefully. As I spoke, I focused on the back of the class to avoid the stares, a trick given to me last year by Mr. Washington, my English teacher. I recited my text at full speed, eager to get it over with and finally be able to sit down at my desk in safety. I was already out of breath.

I only blanked one time, but fortunately my text was nearby. I quickly got back on track with my presentation. Once I finished my text, I received a polite round of applause and returned to my seat with relief. I took a deep breath. I thought I had done pretty well.

When Christian introduced himself to the class, my heart raced. I tried to hide my fascination with him. As I glanced around discreetly, I noticed I was not the only girl who seemed charmed by his beauty. Several of my companions were staring at him, silly smiles plastered to their lips. I took advantage of their preoccupation with him and turned my eyes onto the object of my lust.

Christian always seemed at ease, even while standing in front of thirty students who were staring at him. He spoke with a disconcerting confidence, despite the many grammatical errors that plagued his speech. He even added a few jokes to his presentation. I was swooning. I expected no less from Christian Davis.

Thunderous applause resounded at the end of his presentation. Christian returned to his seat with a determined, almost arrogant step.

He occupied my thoughts for the rest of the day. I was on cloud nine and couldn't hear anything that was going on around me as I kept replaying his presentation in my head. Like a zombie, I walked around aimlessly, a goofy smile on my face, and collided with two students on their way to the library. I was a victim of the Christian charisma.

At the turn of a corridor, I heard Ashley, Morgan and Caroline talking animatedly.

"Let's do that again. That was awesome!"

"Yes, it was worth it to be so tired today."

I stopped dead in my tracks. This is exactly what they were hiding from me. My heart broke. My best friends—no matter how I'd felt about them lately, they were the best I had—had gone barhopping yesterday without me. *Without even inviting me.*

I was boiling with rage. Gone were the naughty thoughts about Christian. Thoughts of murder replaced them. *Stupid bitches!* How I couldn't wait to graduate and get the hell out of this shitty school with these shitty people. Girls without much ambition and guys who only thought about cars and sex. Who was I? An alien?

A bitter tear rolled down my cheek. I ran off down a hallway to avoid those traitors having the joy of seeing me in this state. I couldn't wait for the end of the year.

I was going on an adventure to leave this quiet, lost, and boring place. I would travel around the world if I had to, but I would find people who were like me, with whom I could develop and maintain enriching friendships.

I sped like a shooting star through the long corridors, which had emptied quickly. It took me two tries to get the combination right on my locker. Even my fingers shook with rage. I threw all my books on the shelf and slammed the door angrily. No way was I going to do homework tonight. I was giving myself the night off to recover. I could never concentrate after what I had just discovered.

I ran headlong out the door. I had no intention of stopping for anyone. *Watch out! If I hit you, it'll be your fault!*

I had barely made it out of the school when I came face-to-face with Brianna. It came as a shock. Seeing her in front of me pulled me from my negative thoughts. She, too, had been betrayed.

By me.

What was she doing there? I was about to find out because she was already opening her mouth, but I didn't want to be seen with her. I had enough problems as it was. So I pulled the hood of my coat down over my head and continued on my way.

She followed me. "Emily. I want to talk to you. Can I walk with you?"

"Yes," I said reluctantly.

Why had my mother taught me good manners? All I wanted was to close that chapter and move on, so I sped up. I wasn't happy about having a confrontation with Brianna a second time. Had I not made myself clear?

However, when I saw she was crying, my heart melted immediately. I slowed my pace and faced her, inviting her to talk to me.

"I don't understand why you don't want to talk to me anymore," Brianna said, sobbing. "I thought we were getting along."

She snuffled. Her eyes were red. I didn't want to admit that my friends had dragged me into this. I didn't want her to think I was that stupid and suggestible. Looking back on the day I had been so cruel to her, I felt ashamed. I didn't know what to do.

Spontaneously, I took her in my arms to comfort her. "Hey,

you want to come over for dinner?"

Surprised—and rightly so—she agreed. I pulled my cell phone out of my pocket to let my mom know I was bringing a friend home. Brianna did the same to tell her aunt that she was having dinner at my house. We both got the green light.

Brianna followed me. I wasn't very comfortable walking next to her, and I wasn't sure how to react or what to say. An awkward silence hung over us during the walk. I was already regretting my move. What had I gotten myself into? I didn't want the girls to find out.

I had to find something to talk about, anything to break the silence. Anything. We passed the cemetery on our way to my house. I seized the opportunity. "I love cemeteries! They're so cool."

"Yeah?" asked Brianna skeptically.

"A cemetery is so peaceful. It's the perfect place to reflect. Sometimes, I walk around and inspect the tombstones. The oldest one is from 1815."

"I'd love to have you show me around sometime."

Uneasy, I remained silent. It was hard to refuse, so I said nothing. I preferred not to go too far down that slippery slope because the future of our friendship seemed impossible.

Relieved, I finally saw that we had arrived at my house. At least I had carried on a conversation until we reached our destination. I pushed open the white door. The whole family was waiting for us, and I introduced them to Brianna.

"Mom, Dad, this is Brianna."

Brianna walked toward them, her hand outstretched. At a glance, I knew that her particular look surprised my parents. She wore a white cotton blouse and a long burlap skirt. Feathers adorned her braided hair, which fell to her shoulders.

Thankfully, they didn't comment on her appearance, which saved me from feeling ashamed. The indulgent look my parents exchanged with each other perplexed me. It could mean that they thought we were in our "teenager phase," as my mother liked to say. For once, I didn't get upset since my parents wouldn't ask questions I didn't want to face.

My father was the first to warmly shake Brianna's hand. "Welcome to our home, Brianna. I am Stephen, and this is my wife, Laura."

My mother smiled at her. "It's a pleasure to meet you. I hope you like pasta."

Brianna nodded.

Lillian was jumping around with gusto. She wanted to show Brianna her room and her toys. She tugged insistently on Brianna's sleeve to motivate her. Brianna agreed to accompany her until supper, which temporarily calmed my sister's over-heated temperament. To my surprise, Lillian seemed charmed by Brianna. If only my friends could have loved her, too, my life would be so much easier. That thought left me wondering.

"Let's eat!" my mother said.

We left the dolls on the floor of Lillian's room and hurried into the dining room. A steaming bowl of pasta carbonara sat on the table. The room smelled delicious. I sat Brianna down beside me. Hungry, I filled my plate with garlic bread au gratin, pasta, and Caesar salad. *Yummy!*

Dinner went off without a hitch. We seemed like a perfectly normal family, chatting and laughing as we passed the dishes and salt shaker around. My family had quickly come to appreciate Brianna's true personality, beyond her unsettling looks.

Dinner ended with delicious slices of sugar pie and scoops of vanilla ice cream. My parents gave me the day off from doing the dishes so I could take care of my guest. That was great. We slipped away into the basement, and I was thrilled to get out of the chores I normally had to do. We sat comfortably on my bed and chatted nonstop. Brianna always had something funny to say.

During the evening, we discussed everything and anything with a baffling spontaneity, and I even told her about my fantasy about Christian Davis.

"You have a crush on Christian?" she asked. "You know he's in my gym class?"

"Really? You're lucky. So, how is he? I'm sure he's strong."

"What a guy!"

Of course, she had also noticed Christian. He was a hunk, I swear.

"I'm sure he is great to look at on the field," I said.

Brianna confirmed my impression. "Yesterday in PE, he spiked the volleyball so hard it went down like a bomb. The opposing team didn't even try to intercept it. They were too scared."

I was swooning just hearing Brianna describe his great agility, and I kept asking her for more details while drinking in her words. I was hooked, but I was wasting my time. He was in love with Maria. *Bad luck!*

Suddenly, the day I'd told Brianna to stop bothering my friends and me came back to mind. I felt the need to set the record straight. I couldn't keep pretending that nothing had happened. Her tears were still weighing on my heart.

"You know, Brianna, our conversation the other day in the cafeteria… I really didn't mean to upset you."

"Don't worry," Brianna said, holding her hand out in front

of my face as a sign to stop. "I get it. Your friends don't want me around. That's why I wanted to talk to you today. I wanted to explain to you I don't mind. I'm fine with being alone at school."

Surprised by this revelation, I let her continue. "You know, I've often had a hard time making friends with all my moving around. Plus, I don't like to waste my time on superficial conversations. Your friends are not my style at all."

I nodded. I knew exactly what she meant.

"That's why I think we understand each other," Brianna said. "Could we talk only outside of school? I'd like that."

She looked at me with imploring eyes. I thought for a few seconds about her proposal. It seemed hypocritical to ignore her during class and hang out with her afterward... but it was her idea after all, so why not take advantage of it? I would have the best of both worlds.

"Okay, deal," I said, shaking her hand to make our agreement official.

She shook my hand enthusiastically.

"Come on, give me your cell phone number so I can text you."

We exchanged phone numbers. She added her details in my contact list, and I added mine to hers. We looked at each other and smiled. I threw a pillow at her, laughing, and we bickered. Finally, I felt my boring routine had been broken. Meeting my new secret friend would spice up my life.

Brianna left early in the evening. Time had flown by, as I had really enjoyed myself with her. I hadn't felt this good in a long time and had to admit that Brianna was a wonderful friend. No more pretending. I felt understood and accepted. I could be myself, authentic without fear of being judged. It was only when I took off the mask that I realized how heavy it was.

I grabbed my diary to record the highlights of the evening. As Brianna and I had discussed, I ignored her all week at school. The students didn't even notice her anymore—she had become part of the furniture. Sitting at our usual table, I noticed my friends had also quickly forgotten about her. None of them seemed to feel any remorse at all about putting Brianna aside. I found them downright petty. They were losing a little more of my esteem every day.

As I sat at the table, I looked forward to finishing high school and finally getting them out of my life for good. I had two more years to put up with this charade.

On Thursday, I felt my cell phone vibrate in my pocket. I checked my text messages. It was Brianna who had texted me.

See you on Friday? :) :)

Why not? I quickly typed a reply as the bell was already ringing for the start of school.

After school, I intended to hasten home but stopped for a few minutes at the cemetery to enjoy a few moments of quiet.

I walked along the unkempt grass paths. Dead leaves were already covering the ground in some places. The wind whistled between the tombstones. I was taking deep breaths, almost in meditation, when someone suddenly appeared.

"Ah!" I screamed.

"You need to learn to relax, girl! Otherwise, you won't last long."

Brianna stood before me, roaring with laughter.

"You'd be scared, too, if a crazy woman jumped out at you in a graveyard," I said, chuckling.

I threw a few dead leaves at her, and we rolled around laughing on the cold, wet ground. Out of breath and holding my ribs, I ended the hostilities. Catching my breath, I asked her, "What are you doing here?"

"I've been curious about the cemetery since we walked by it when I went to your house for dinner," Brianna said. "I wanted to see what you were talking about. It's true that it's peaceful, even with the icy wind."

"Yes, but only when no one is attacking you from behind."

"I have to go home. My aunt is waiting for me. See you tomorrow!"

The next day was Friday, the day we'd agreed I would come to Brianna's aunt's house directly after school. My parents had given me their permission, and I was curious to see the inside of the house.

I knew where she lived with her aunt. The house had always aroused my curiosity. It had especially stimulated my imagination. The house seemed to be shrouded in a veil of mystery, as if a perpetual fog refused to dissipate. Its architecture differed from that of the surrounding houses. The white paint had faded and peeled in some places. A small angular roof decorated the narrow front. The interior always seemed dark as the habitants kept the curtains shut. Two huge red oaks that must have been a hundred years old stood in the front yard, partly hiding the dwelling. Their imposing trunks formed ominous shadows.

The prospect of meeting Brianna's aunt worried me a little. She must be quite impressive to have such a special house.

As planned, Brianna was waiting for me at the end of class. We'd agreed to meet at the back of the school so as not to attract attention. We walked down the path together. I pulled up the collar of my jacket and shoved my hands into my pockets. The end of September was approaching, and the autumn wind was blowing on us.

Brianna lived near the school. It took us only a few minutes to walk the distance. When we arrived at her aunt's house, she pushed open the door. Although I had expected an original setting, nothing had prepared me for this vision.

The interior of the ancestral home was indeed dark. Curtains partially hid the small windows. Shelves covered all the walls, overflowing with pots, rusty metal boxes, old leather-bound books, and dried herbs. The sight intrigued me. The sheer number of objects seemed to be arranged in an order that I could not understand. I went forward to examine more closely the items piled on the shelves. I dared not touch anything. As I explored, I found a crystal ball as large as a bowling ball. Resting on a sturdy base of polished metal, the sphere glowed with an eerie light. Why was Brianna's aunt accumulating such strange things?

Brianna paid no attention to my curiosity. She casually tossed her bag onto the front bench and kicked off her shoes. I guessed she was used to her aunt's decorative style. After all, she had been living with her for two weeks. Besides, she was pretty amazing herself.

Brianna invited me to look around the house. I realized with embarrassment that, in my fascination, I had kept my shoes on. My mother would have blushed with shame at my lack of politeness. So I hurriedly took them off and followed Brianna. She went to the refrigerator and took out two boxes of grapefruit juice. I took the one she handed me. The rest of the house was as cluttered as the entrance. I felt as if I had entered a parallel universe.

Brianna's room was on the second floor. I followed her, and we went up a narrow, steep staircase, almost like a ladder. It was typical of a century-old house. To keep my balance, I put my hands on the steps. At the end, Brianna lifted a large trap door. We ended up in the attic. Her room was there. The roof beams were visible, and the walls were bare, but freshly refinished hardwood covered the floor. *What a splendid room! I was green with envy.*

Her bed was at the back of the room, near the only window, which was small and square. Brianna was not as well organized as her aunt. Open books, candy wrappers, and crumpled clothes were strewn about the room. She kicked some items away as she made her way to her bed. She bounced and fell onto it.

I was uncomfortable with the mess. I crossed the room without looking at the floor to make sure I didn't discover any underwear on my way. Unlike Brianna, I liked structured, tidy, uncluttered spaces. Everything in my room was neatly arranged.

About three times a year, I emptied the contents of my drawers and wardrobe on my bed to take inventory. I didn't hesitate to get rid of anything I no longer needed. Each time, I felt great satisfaction. My mind seemed freer when I knew I had only what I needed—nothing more, nothing less. I found it easier to find my favorite possessions that way. Brianna obviously did not.

I decided I didn't need to share my obsession with tidying up with Brianna. Still, I promised myself that I would encourage her to clean up her mess later. For today, I was content to sit next to her on the bed, making sure I didn't put my butt on anything important—or disgusting—beforehand.

I had to be home by nine o'clock. At sixteen, I felt my parents should allow me to stay out longer. However, this time the curfew benefited me. It was my first visit to Brianna's house, and I had a ready-made excuse to leave if we didn't get along as well as I thought we would. I intended to negotiate intensely for an extension of my curfew at the next opportunity.

Brianna said to me, "Have you read the paper? There was an article about uniforms. How awful!"

She was, of course, talking about the school newspaper, a monthly publication produced by the students. The Parent Council was considering introducing uniforms, the most recent controversy at the school.

It delighted me to hear Brianna's arguments against the uniforms. Finally, a substantive debate rather than superficial and futile conversations. We both agreed that we had no intention of accepting ugly uniforms. Our clothes allowed us to express ourselves, to show the world who we were. I could understand that parents hoped to eliminate discrimination and bullying. However, those who liked to laugh at others would always find reasons to make fun of them. If students were all in uniforms, the bullies would just find something besides clothes to criticize in their victims.

Speaking of teasing, the students had teased Brianna for the first few days following her arrival, but it hadn't lasted very long. For some mysterious reason, those who had bullied her had quickly lost all pleasure in harassing her. They ignored her now, which was fortunate for her. I had heard too many stories of young girls becoming anorexic or developing other self-esteem problems under the onslaught of taunts.

The conversation took an unexpected turn to a discussion of unexplained phenomena. My rational mind told me that any-thing that could not be explained scientifically was nonsense, but my childish heart clung to the idea—the hope—that magic could indeed exist. Unexplained phenomena fascinated me.

I had consulted a few books on white magic and tried a few experiments, but without the desired effect. As for aliens, I did not believe that Earth could be the only planet in the universe that contained life.

Brianna told me she was particularly interested in magic. Something clicked in my mind. All the jars and herbs I'd seen in the kitchen and in the living room as well as the candles and incense were objects that could be used in magical rituals.

"You really don't believe in magic?" Brianna asked.

"I might have tried a few times to reproduce a spell that would make me rich and beautiful. Without result, as you can see," I said.

Brianna moved closer to me and lowered her voice. "Emily, I'm going to tell you a secret, but you must promise not to reveal it to anyone. Not to your friends, not to your parents, not to your sister, not to any stranger even on the other side of the world."

I nodded in curiosity. She had a conspiratorial air about her. Was I finally going to learn why Brianna was so scheming?

"I'm staying with my aunt to learn more about magic," she said in my ear, as if we were being bugged.

Her revelation stunned me. I held back from bursting out laughing. Was she really serious? I didn't know what to say. So, Brianna was an enlightened person who believed in white magic. It was only out of curiosity that most people bought those magical recipe books. No one in their right mind would believe in such nonsense.

Embarrassed, I didn't know how to react or how to get out of this mess. I glanced discreetly at my watch. With relief, I saw that there were only a few minutes left before my curfew. My rational mind took over. All I had to do was pretend I believed her. In a few minutes, I would leave, and I would just have to avoid her until she left me alone. For once, my friends had been right.

"That's cool," I replied, pretending to be as enthusiastic as possible.

I hoped she wouldn't decode the condescending tone of my remark.

"Don't be condescending," she said in a harsh tone.

Oops.

"I can prove to you what I say," Brianna said. "Ask me anything, and I will grant your wish."

With her arms crossed over her chest, she challenged me with her eyes. No need to pretend to believe her anymore. She had immediately seen through my game. With nothing left to lose, I didn't hesitate to taunt her. "World peace?"

"All right. Hilarious. I admit my powers are not that great, nor will they ever be. Ask me to do something closer to home, like school."

Thinking for a few seconds, I had no trouble figuring out what to wish for—that Christian and Maria would separate and that he would become interested in me. My conscience wasn't clear at the thought of making the wish, but since there would be no consequences, I might as well dream a little. I was going to shut up this so-called witch's apprentice.

"I want Christian to leave Maria and ask me out," I said, defiantly and decidedly. "That is my wish."

Far from being discouraged, Brianna smiled.

"Very good," she said, rubbing her hands together in satisfaction.

Her confidence did nothing to reassure me of her mental state. She grabbed an old leather-bound book from her bedside table and quickly scanned the table of contents. Obviously, she found what she was looking for and closed the book with a snap. She cleared the center of the room, using her feet to send the clothes lying around flying, revealing a pentagram drawn in white chalk on the floor.

Then she rummaged around the room, gathering the tools she needed for her spell. She placed them in the pentagram as she went. She gathered a half-melted white candle, matches, a glass plate—like the ones my mother used to bake her pies—a dried maple leaf, a felt pen, scissors, incense, and a needle.

She lit the candle and placed it on the glass plate. At least she was taking precautions not to set the house on fire. She invited me to join her in the center of the room and indicated a spot on the floor, near the pentagram. It felt ridiculous to play her game, but it still intrigued me. I had wished for more spice in my life, and I was getting it.

Brianna turned off the light. She sat cross-legged in front of me then lit the incense stick with the candle. A smell of wild roses filled the room. She muttered a few words that sounded like a prayer as she sent smoke in four directions. The points of the compass?

She put the incense back next to the candle, safely on the glass plate. I felt a little more reassured. Still, I was curious and wanted to see what would happen next.

Brianna picked up the maple leaf and placed it over the stick of flowery incense. She rolled the stem between her fingers to swirl the leaf and infuse it with the fragrant smoke. Then she placed it on the floor and picked up the felt-tip pen. She wrote *Christian* on one half and *Maria* on the other. The candlelight flickered, casting eerie shadows on the walls and on Brianna's face. She had a concentrated pout. The whole thing amazed me. She really believed in magic.

She took the needle between her fingers and passed it through the flame several times to disinfect it. Now I was not at all reassured. What did she want with a needle? Did she intend to use her blood?

She held out her hand to me. I realized in a flash that it was my blood she wanted to use, but it was too late to back out. With reluctance, I held out my hand. She took it. I extended my index finger and turned away apprehensively. I was hot. She pricked me ever so slightly, just enough to squeeze out two tiny drops of blood from my fingertip. She wiped them in turn under the names on the maple leaf.

Satisfied, she gave me the scissors. She showed me with her finger where to cut in the middle of the leaf to get two symmetrical pieces and thus separate the names of Christian and Maria. I did so. She took Maria's piece and passed it over the flame to burn it. She handed me the second half. I thought I should burn that, too, so I moved it closer to the flame. She quickly stopped me.

"No. Keep it. You'll see the result."

She blew out the candle and extinguished the incense. Then she turned on the ceiling light again, and the light dazzled me. The real world grabbed me. I'd been caught up in her nonsense, but now that the light was back to normal, I realized how ridiculous the situation was. I wanted to leave as soon as possible.

I looked at my watch and mumbled to Brianna that I had to go. I was already late. *Shit.* I walked down the stairs trying to act calm, but I wanted to get out of the house and away from Brianna and her madness quickly. I grabbed my backpack and hurriedly slipped on my shoes. At least I had the excuse of being late, so I didn't need to linger. A quick wave to Brianna, and I was off.

I walked at a steady pace to the house. Fortunately, the weather was not too cold. I closed the door of the house behind me with relief. I threw my bag on the hall floor and headed to my room after calling a quick "Good night" to my parents. Captivated by a TV show, they didn't seem too concerned about my being a few minutes late. I was relieved that I didn't have to talk to them. I couldn't pretend that everything was normal, and they would have smelled it, like a dog smells fear.

Sitting safely on my bed, I opened my hand. I hadn't realized I was still holding the half of the maple leaf with Christian's name on it. Lying on my bed, I looked at it. The drop of my blood had left a strange mark, almost in the shape of a heart, although I could be hallucinating because of recent events.

I placed the maple leaf between the pages of my diary. I didn't know why I kept it even though it repulsed me. As soon as I closed my diary, I erased its existence from my mind.

Discovering I had been wrong about Brianna made me feel depressed. I thought I had finally found a friend I could count on, with whom I could share everything and who could do the same with me. Sadly, I'd been mistaken. My loneliness hit me hard.

Would life get easier? It seemed like with every passing year, it got more complicated. I picked up my phone and turned on Spotify in an attempt to build an impenetrable bubble around me. I was grieving.

I was alone in the world, a strange beast stranded among human beings whose beliefs, functioning, and language I did not understand. I could only fit in by wearing a mask that was weighing me down. How much longer could I stand it?

Exhausted, I fell asleep, my eyes reddened by burning tears of disappointment.

Chapter 4

The next morning, I resolved to put that awful evening with Brianna behind me. Life was too short to waste on self-pity, right? There was no point in moping around.

In just two years, I would finish high school and be able to study away from here.

I had to make the most of the time left before going to college.

It was Saturday. I was playing tennis with my mother that afternoon. It was our exclusive mother-daughter quality time. Tennis was the only sport I could play. I was a complete failure at everything else.

I couldn't focus on the game. Balls would graze me. I was slow to react. I even dropped my racket, and it flew over the net. My mother beat me to the punch. I was sweating.

On the way home, my mother questioned me. She had noticed that I wasn't feeling well. When she came up against my grumbling and vague answers, she wisely left me alone to brood.

On Monday morning, I arrived at school exhausted. I wondered if I could make it through the day. I made my way to my first class, which was science. At least there was one good thing to start the day—the teacher was easy on the eyes.

All the students wanted to have Martin Thompson as a teacher. I had even seen Lucy make eyes at him and bat her eyelashes. But I knew he had a wife and was far too professional to have any kind of relationship with a student. Still, several students had tried their best tricks, without success.

The teacher looked great this morning, unlike me. I had large, gray circles under my eyes.

"We are going to the provincial crystal-forming competition," he announced cheerfully. "This is the twentieth edition, and I'm looking forward to making it to the finals with you. The top two teams will represent our school in Montreal with their crystals, so do your best."

I did not know what he was talking about. How to *make* and *grow* a crystal? I paid attention to his explanation of how the competition would work. I used to enter many contests, and this one was coming just in time. It would take my mind off things and maybe get me to Montreal.

Excited, Mr. Thompson walked up and down the aisles in the classroom, explaining the procedure to us.

"The process is simple. To begin, you need to prepare a solution of water and salt. This year, the salt to use is copper sulfate pentahydrate. Once the solution is prepared, deposits will build up at the bottom. We will harvest the best specimen next class.

"We will then suspend them in a beaker filled with the salt solution. The work will only begin at this point. But I will tell you more when we get there. For now, we'll just prepare the solution."

The experiment sounded interesting, but I didn't really like teamwork. With little enthusiasm, I turned around to see who I could team up with. I realized I was too late—all the other students had already formed their teams. The only person free was at the back of the class… Brianna. Why was I so unlucky? It was like a curse. I didn't want to end up working with her. I already had goose bumps.

"Does everyone have a partner?" Mr. Thompson asked. "Good. Come and get the instruction sheet from my table. The bags of copper sulfate pentahydrate are here at the front, and the rest of the equipment is in the cupboards by the door."

All the students got up and settled into a joyful cacophony. I walked over to Brianna. I said to her, "I'll take care of the bag. You take care of the rest."

She nodded. She seemed more excited than I was about the idea of teaming up. We sat down at the back of the classroom. I carefully read the instruction sheet prepared by our teacher. The first step was to boil the distilled water. Then I diluted an impressive amount of salt in the water. Brianna was checking my every move.

"So, no news from Christian?" Brianna asked.

I'm not going down that slippery slope. We need to get this assignment done.

"Brianna, I need to focus. I really want to get through this experiment."

"Okay," she said, sounding disappointed.

Once the solution was ready, I poured it into a beaker. All that remained was to wait for the first salt crystals to form. The class was already over, and I hurried to put the equipment away.

On Tuesday, at the next class, I went straight to our beaker to find that tiny crystals had settled in the bottom overnight. Satisfied, I took my seat. The bell announced the start of class, and all the students took their seats.

"So, are you excited?" Mr. Thompson asked. "Today we are going to do the most critical part of the process. Now we have to choose the crystal that is closest to the shape we want. Here is a picture of what your crystal should look like."

The projector showed a magnified image of copper sulfate pentahydrate.

"Empty your beakers and examine your crystals," Mr. Thompson said. "Select them carefully according to size and shape. Afterward, you will need to hang your crystal in a beaker refilled with the salt and water solution. Oversaturation will cause particles to accumulate on all sides of your crystal."

We re-formed our teams. I was eager to see the results. I carefully emptied the solution to get out the crystals, my babies.

"Brianna, look at these and pick the three best ones," I said. "I will do the same, and then we can choose the best one."

"Good idea!"

I meticulously examined my half of the small crystals of copper sulfate pentahydrate one by one, comparing them with the photo projected on the wall. I selected three that looked promising.

Mr. Thompson circulated among the teams. "So, girls, did you find our next winner?"

I showed him our six best crystals.

"Very good," he said. "I recommend you use this one. Even though it's a little smaller, it has the perfect shape."

Convinced, we suspended the crystal in the solution with a tiny thread. No sooner had we finished than the class was over. We had to hurry and put our equipment away before going out for a break. The teacher shouted over the din the students were making to tell us we could come in at lunchtime to take care of our crystal.

"Replacing oversaturated water frequently will promote crystal growth," Mr. Thompson said. "Also it will filter out impurities and rework the shape to avoid imperfections."

Since I wasn't very good at sports, my competitive spirit had to show up in other areas. Besides, I would not pass up the opportunity to see the handsome Mr. Thompson more often. I took good care of my crystal by checking it regularly. I doubted Brianna would show up, as she didn't seem to take the experiment too seriously.

But I was not counting on my notorious bad luck. The next day at noon, when I pushed open the classroom door, she was already at the station, preparing a new solution. She turned around when she heard me enter. I couldn't leave now that she had seen me. Besides, I didn't want to run away. I had to prove my courage.

This activity was forcing me to collaborate with her and get to know her even better. Each time, her powerful thoughts, her candor, and her sense of humor charmed me. She always said that if you want to leave your mark, avoid walking in the footsteps of others. *What a philosophy!* Was there such a thing as love at first sight? Because, despite everything I had discovered about Brianna, I could not help but be her friend. And the feeling was mutual. We had a great time meeting up in the classroom at lunchtime. There was no way my friends would see us here together as they had no interest in this project.

On Fridays, I had my Spanish class with Christian. He'd been acting really weird lately. He smiled at me several times when I ran into him this week, and I caught him looking at me several times during class. Had the tide finally turned in my favor? The girls told me he broke up with Maria on Monday morning. The delight with which Ashley told me about Maria's crying fit disgusted me. Since then, Maria had been walking around with her head down and her eyes red. She didn't even wear makeup anymore. I felt a little sorry for her, but it was good news for me.

That meant Christian was free now.

When the bell rang, I gathered my books and stood up quickly. Not looking where I was going, I ran straight into Christian and dropped all my books. He bent down to help me pick them up as the classroom emptied.

"Sorry," I said, confused.

"No problem. I'm the one who came forward to talk to you."

I blushed. Christian wanted to talk to me? Why did he want to talk to me? I realized that I had stopped breathing. I had to force air to enter my lungs.

"Ah…" I said, smiling at him in a goofy way.

"I'd like to take you out to dinner tomorrow. I mean, if you're free."

"Yes!"

A little too quick an answer. Hadn't I fantasized enough about this day that I could have come up with a more intelligent, sensual, interesting line? As usual, the perfect line would probably come to me later in the day.

Christian seemed delighted. He dazzled me with his beautiful, white-toothed smile.

"Great, I'll pick you up at six. Do you like the Italiani restaurant?"

I would have agreed to eat at a dump if that was where he suggested. But Italiani was the most upscale restaurant in town. I was in a state. My legs felt like cotton wool. I put my hand on the table behind me to restrain myself. I was trying to hide my excitement.

The only answer I could manage was "Yes!"

An eloquent example of originality on my part. He turned and walked away, smiling. I had completely frozen, behaving like a complete idiot. I had to come up with a list of topics for the evening, because I didn't want to improvise in front of Christian. He was blowing my mind, and I wasn't trusting my brain to come up with something clever to say. After all, it had just failed me badly.

The bell for the next class woke me from my reverie. I rushed to my locker to get my books for my art class. On my way to class, I passed Brianna. I couldn't resist telling her the news. Since we were supposed to be ignoring each other, she had been about to walk right past me without a glance. I was desperate to talk to her, so I stopped her by taking her arm. She turned around.

"Brianna! Christian invited me! We're going to Italiani's for dinner tomorrow!" I said, trying not to scream with joy.

I didn't want to draw attention to us, let alone alarm the entire school.

"So it worked!" she said, winking at me and continuing on her way.

I was speechless. The second bell rang. I was late for class. I ran toward my classroom. Out of breath, I floundered into my chair.

I could not concentrate. In a few words, Brianna had completely shattered my enthusiasm. A terrible doubt crept into my mind. Was Christian really interested in me, or was he under Brianna's spell? It was impossible. Magic certainly didn't exist. But for Christian to drop Maria and suddenly ask me out was unlikely. Yet it had happened.

I heard nothing the teacher said. The bell finally rang,

signaling the end of class. I got up like a robot, walking without noticing my surroundings or participating in any conversations.

Lying on my bed at home a short time later, I made a decision. I was going to enjoy every moment of my evening with Christian. I had dreamed about him for so long that I needed to seize this opportunity. And even if he was interested in me simply because of Brianna's spell, I was convinced that I could seduce him for real with my personality. All he needed was a little push to notice me. I relegated doubts to a corner of my subconscious and decided not to think about them anymore.

By Saturday night, I was in a state. I had really struggled to figure out what to wear. The clothes I had tried on covered my bed. My reflection in the mirror was decent. I had pulled my thick hair up into a sophisticated, loose bun. A few curls were brushing my face. I was wearing a black skirt and a gray top with gray lace sleeves. On my pedicured feet, I had slipped on the delicate sandals I had worn to my cousin's wedding the previous summer. I put on a little makeup, but not too much. I didn't want to look like a desperate girl going all out either. Long silver earrings completed my ensemble.

The doorbell rang. I had butterflies in my stomach. There was no time to hesitate about my look. I grabbed my black satchel with alacrity and rushed to answer the door, climbing the stairs from my downstairs bedroom two at a time. I arrived just in time. My father was already opening the door for Christian. I had no desire to have him subjected to a full-scale interrogation. It would be too embarrassing.

Taking Christian by the arm, I said a brief "good evening" to my father without turning around while ushering Christian out the door. First blunder avoided.

Christian had borrowed his father's car for the event, a black Mercedes convertible parked at the end of the driveway. Beautiful and rich. I whistled in admiration at the vehicle.

"I spent all day polishing it!" Christian said.

He went around the car to open the door for me. It was romantic. I got in, and he hurried to his seat. My hands were sweaty from nervousness. I wiped them discreetly on the fabric of my skirt. The silence in the cabin was heavy, making me doubly nervous. I had to think of something to say. The entire list of ideas I had mentally prepared had faded from my mind. I fell back on the first question that came to me. "So—"

"What do you think—"

We had talked at the same time. An even more embarrassing moment.

"What did you say?" I asked.

"Ah, hey… What do you think of my dad's car?"

"Great! It's great!"

Bravo! What an impressive display of eloquence. I held back from slapping myself on the forehead. It didn't look promising for the rest of the evening.

At the restaurant, the server seated us at a round table covered with a classy white tablecloth. We were in a quiet corner, and the discreet light of a small candle flickered, creating shadows on Christian's delicious face. After the first moments of discomfort, I relaxed a little, and the conversation became much more fluid.

The meal was delectable, and Christian was pleasant company. By the time dessert arrived, I was laughing out loud. Christian's eyes were shining. He was even more irresistible for it.

At the end of the evening, I stood in front of the door of my house and looked into his beautiful eyes. Without thinking about it, I leaned in to give him a kiss. He didn't hesitate to kiss me back. I felt myself melting with happiness.

"Good night," he said, stroking my cheek.

I smiled at him. He got back in the car and started it up. *Whew! What a perfect evening!* My cheeks hurt from smiling so much. I walked silently back into the house. My parents were watching television in the living room.

"So?" asked my mother, unable to contain her curiosity.

"I had a great time!" I said.

I had no intention of saying anything else. I was in too much of a hurry to get to my diary to record every detail of the evening because I didn't want to forget any second of it.

I ran into my room, chased by my cat. I let him in and closed the door. Promptly, I took my diary from my drawer and unlocked it before sitting on my bed, my cat purring at my side while I recounted the whole evening in detail. As I told my story, my enthusiasm waned. Brianna's words came back to me. They haunted me. What if Christian wasn't really interested in me? What if Brianna's spell had caused him to pay attention to me? I didn't want to live a false, forced love. I wanted to feel loved for my true self, with my qualities and flaws. Artificial love had nothing to do with it.

I retrieved the maple leaf half from the last page of my journal. As I lay in bed, I turned the situation over in my mind. I concluded that there was only one solution. I had to ask Brianna to break the spell. Only then would I know if Christian loved me for me or not. Once she performed the ceremony to undo her spell, I would only have to see Christian's reaction to know how he really felt about me.

How could I not have thought of this before? Once I had made the decision, I could easily fall asleep.

The following Monday, I went and looked after my crystal during the lunch break. I suspected Brianna would be there as well and that I would tell her my plan. As expected, she arrived at the same time as I did. We distilled the water on the stove, then I took a deep breath and started.

"Brianna, I need you to reverse the spell you cast on Christian."

"Oh yes, that's right. I want you to tell me all the details of your evening with him. Given your request, I imagine it did not go as planned."

"No, no, it's not what you think. He was very kind." I smiled as I recalled my evening. "He made me laugh so hard. I think we have a lot in common. We even kissed on my doorstep! He is such a good kisser! His lips are really soft and warm."

My eyes sparkled at the memory. Brianna's eyes, however, were not filled with stars like mine. Instead, they were full of question marks.

"What's up? Why do you want me to break the spell? I don't understand it."

Her cynicism brought me down to earth. Should I share my doubts with her? Absentmindedly, I shuffled the chemical solution. I didn't want to hear her confirm that Christian would dump me once she broke the spell. I liked to think he'd still like me afterward, and I didn't want to lose hope. No. I preferred to keep my thoughts to myself.

Brianna was still waiting for my answer.

"It's my choice," I said abruptly, hoping she wouldn't pursue the subject any further.

"Very well," she said in an excited tone. "There's no need to get upset!"

"Thank you," I said, returning to our crystal.

I wanted to solve this problem as soon as possible, and I proposed that I come to her house tonight. She agreed.

"Don't forget to bring half a maple leaf with Christian's name on it," she said. "I'll need it."

It was a good thing I'd kept it. I arrived at her house after supper. Brianna opened the door for me. In a hurry to get it over with, I pushed Brianna up the stairs to her room. She had already gathered her props on the floor. The pentagram was clearly visible. Like last time, she lit a candle and motioned for me to take my place on the floor. When we were face-to-face, with the candle between us, she lit the incense stick. I noticed that this incense did not smell like the one from the first time. The pleasant smell reminded me of a coniferous forest in spring. Anxiety overtook me.

"Brianna, don't forget that I just want to undo the spell, not make Christian hate me."

"Don't worry. This isn't the first time I've dissolved a spell." She seemed upset by my doubts. "Did you bring the leaf?"

I nodded. I took it out of my purse and placed it on the floor. Satisfied, she sent the smoke from the incense stick in four directions. As she did this, she recited an incantation. She took the maple leaf half and placed it in her palm. With the thumb of her other hand, she crushed the leaf with vigorous circular movements. The poor dried leaf crackled in her hand into a thousand little pieces. She closed her hand over the dust.

Brianna stood up. I didn't move, fearing that a false move would interfere with the process. Brianna walked over to the only window in the room and opened it wide. She stuck her hand through the opening and unfolded her fingers. A gust of wind lifted the particles in her palm. She turned back to me, looking satisfied.

"That's it! It's done. I just hope you don't regret the opportunity I gave you with Christian."

"I'll live with the consequences, whatever they are," I said grumpily.

"Blow out the candle, will you?"

I blew on it. Relieved, I stood up. At least I hadn't had to contribute blood this time. A shiver of disgust ran down my spine at the memory.

"Thank you, Brianna. I have to go now."

Brianna looked disappointed that I was leaving so early but nodded. She walked me to the door. I put my shoes back on.

"See you tomorrow," I said as I stepped through the doorway.

She waved and closed the door behind me.

I walked, my heart feeling light. I had made the right choice and was ready to face the consequences.

On Tuesday morning, I sat at our usual table with my friends. The incessant hubbub of students enjoying the break before class made me dizzy. My ears rang. I couldn't concentrate on the girls' conversation. I hadn't seen Christian yet, and I couldn't stand not knowing his feelings for me. I wanted to know if he was still interested in me. Butterflies churned in my stomach.

As I walked to my locker, I saw him talking to his friends. His eyes locked with mine. With hope, I gave him my best smile as I walked toward him. He responded to my smile with embarrassment and spun to his friends. He spoke loudly and engaged in a conversation meant to exclude me. Message received.

I turned and bowed my head. I didn't want to humiliate

myself any further. His non-verbal language had already told me everything, and I would have had to be blind to ignore it. I felt my eyes fill with tears. No crying here.

Flushed, I rushed to my locker to get my books. I would double down on my studies to try not to think about Christian. I would have plenty of time to feel sorry for myself tonight in my room, out of sight, and to empty the well in my eyes.

It was easier said than done. My classes were deadly boring, and I couldn't stop my mind from wandering. I turned over every event in my head. I could see every movement of the clock hand in slow motion. *Tick, tiick, tiiick...* Sweat was beading on my forehead. To keep busy, I started a major art project in my planner. I frantically colored in all the little squares that I had traced out so meticulously.

By lunchtime, I couldn't take it anymore. For the first time in my life, I decided to skip class and go home. I almost ran on the way home, feeling tears sting my eyes.

I unlocked the front door of my house in a hurry and entered. Quickly, I sent my shoes flying with two agile kicks and ran to my room. Once again, I pulled my diary out of my drawer, turned on my music, and sat down on my bed. I felt a visceral need to get my feelings out and put them on paper to make myself feel better. I opened the notebook to the right page. My hand froze in the air, my pencil motionless. I couldn't see. Tears filled my eyes and rolled down my cheeks. I threw myself on my bed and cried warmly against my pillow. Enzo the cat came to me and purred beside my face. His presence comforted me a little. I held him close to my heart and petted him. The tears were flowing less now, but they did not dry up. My heart was so heavy.

Once again, I went back to my journal and poured out

my pain on its pages. I had to put words to my pain, so I straightened up and positioned myself cross-legged, placing Enzo on my folded legs. I took my pencil and scribbled down everything that came to mind.

After an hour of frantically filling in the lined pages, I became tired. All the trying emotions had drained me of all my energy. Overwhelmed, I lay my head on the pillow. I hoped that sleep would bring me some comfort.

I didn't wake until my mother arrived. She found me lying on my bed.

"Emily! What are you doing here?" my mother said to wake me up.

She sat on the edge of the bed and shook me lightly.

"Weren't you at school today?" she asked incredulously. "Are you sick?"

Already she was pressing the back of her hand against my forehead. Her understanding voice comforted me. She knew I must have had a good reason for missing class because it was unusual for me. I felt the tears welling up.

"It's Christian," I said, wiping my puffy eyes. "He's not interested in me anymore."

"What do you mean? What happened?"

Excellent question. There must have been a rational explanation. I wasn't about to tell her that Brianna's spell had caused Christian to invite me to dinner, and now that we'd called off the spell, he was no longer interested in me. Yet I'd analyzed every word and movement since my evening with him, and I couldn't find anything that might have displeased him. I really didn't understand boys.

"I don't know," I said frankly.

"Don't worry. When you find the right person, he or she will accept you unconditionally, with your qualities and faults."

"Maybe, but it hurts so much. I hope I never fall in love again!"

I was banging angrily on my feather pillow.

"Don't say that. The only cure for your pain is time. I know it's a cliché, but you'll see that with time, all the pain gets better."

She tucked a lock of hair behind my ear. She was probably right, but what she'd said was the last thing I wanted to hear. My heart was in my throat. She stood beside me for a few moments, patting my back, trying to comfort me. I guess there was nothing else to say. I hadn't thought it was possible to experience such pain.

"Do you want me to bring your dinner to your room?"

I pulled the duvet down over my head and groaned. I was not hungry. My stomach was tightening. My mother understood and left the room. I fell back into a life-saving sleep.

In the middle of the night, my stomach woke me up with an intense gurgling. The memory of Christian immediately came back to me. A bomb of pain exploded inside me and affected all my limbs. My stomach continued to wail, and I finally went upstairs to the kitchen for a bite to eat.

I opened the door to the refrigerator and examined its content, careful not to make any noise. I didn't have to search long. My mother had prepared a small dish filled with leftovers from dinner. *Thanks, Mom!* I put the food in the microwave, hoping that its sound would not wake my parents. My stomach was getting restless. I carefully took out the dish so that the steam wouldn't burn my fingers. I sat down at the silent table and enjoyed my meal. Despite my sadness, life went on. I was now sure of Christian's true feelings for me. The truth was what I'd asked for, despite Brianna's warning. I had to accept the result.

With my belly full, I realized that I really wasn't sleepy anymore. It was understandable. I had slept all afternoon. What could I do to pass the time? Lazily, I walked over to the sofa and turned on the TV. I turned the volume to a minimum, barely loud enough to hear, and I flipped through the infomercials, unable to find a program that would hold my attention.

The next morning, I woke up in the living room. I guess I had dozed off during the *incredible* SuperFlex Turbo cookware offer. I stretched. Already, I was feeling a little better. I knew I'd made the right choice in canceling the spell, even though the consequences were heavy to bear and my heart was aching.

The entire household woke up at the same time. When she saw me on the sofa, my little sister ran to me and took advantage of the fact that I was still lying on the sofa to jump on me and give me a big hug. I gave it back to her happily. My mother came over and smiled when she saw us hugging.

"I think you'll need my foundation this morning, dear. Your face is a mess." She bent down to get a bag of ice from the freezer.

"Put this over your eyes for a moment," my mother said. "It will help with the swelling of your eyes."

I ran to look at myself in the mirror and agreed that I should follow her instructions. I placed the bag over my eyes and waited, hoping to notice the effect soon. Indeed, to my great relief, after a few minutes of treatment, my eyes were more presentable, although they were still red. I put on a little foundation, as my mother had suggested. Already, I looked better. There was no way I was going to give Christian the satisfaction of seeing me in a terrible state.

When I got to school, I gathered the courage to walk through the door. I expected to be bombarded with questions from my friends about my absence, which had surely not gone unnoticed. As I imagined the inquiries that awaited me, I sighed. I might as well face the consequences of my actions right away and move on as soon as possible.

As expected, I had not yet sat down at our table when my friends were already asking me questions.

"Where were you? You missed the video in our history class," Vanessa said.

"You told me you would show me a book in the library. I looked for you, and I couldn't find you anywhere," Joe said.

I sat down and took a deep breath to spout the explanation I had made on the way to school.

"I had a dentist appointment. I had completely forgotten about it. My mother had to call me to remind me, and since I was already late, I left in a hurry."

"Ah, well," Joe said.

The girls seemed disappointed that there was no juicy gossip to get their teeth into. Too bad for them. There was no way I was going to share my disappointment and pain. I didn't want them to find out about my distress and enjoy it. Sure, they already knew I liked Christian, but I had no desire to tell them about the events of the last few days.

In my peripheral vision, I saw Christian with Maria. I watched them discreetly, my heart in pieces. With her arms crossed, she was listening to his plea. From the look on his face, he was begging for her forgiveness and wanted to be her lover again. I turned away sadly. What unnecessary pain I had caused. My stomach tightened with guilt.

At lunchtime, with my tuna sandwich duly eaten, I returned

to the science room to take care of our project. Brianna was already there. I expected her to ask me questions too. To my surprise, she acted as if nothing had happened.

Disconcerted, I wondered why she wasn't curious about what had happened next with Christian. Since she was the only one who knew the complete story, I broached the subject with her, hoping to free myself from my negative feelings.

"I saw Christian again yesterday," I said.

She didn't even turn around. She carefully diluted the crystals of copper sulfate pentahydrate to form the solution. "Hmm."

"He didn't seem to want to talk to me."

"Hmm."

"I must have done something he didn't like. I ruined my chances with him. Yet he kissed me on Friday! I replayed the whole evening in my head repeatedly. This morning he was talking to Maria."

I was talking so fast that I realized I was out of breath.

"Look, Emily." Brianna interrupted me, and I caught my breath. "I didn't want to bring this up again, but since I can see you're concerned about this, I have to be honest with you. Christian isn't interested in you. He's just never been interested in you. It was my spell that caused you to get his attention. You need to accept that and stop dwelling on the past. You have done nothing wrong. Believe in my powers!" Her piercing green eyes looked into mine.

An unpleasant shiver ran down my spine. This girl was scaring the hell out of me.

Chapter 5

The next morning, I was sitting at the table with my friends as usual. With my head resting in the palm of my hand, I pretended to be interested in Morgan's babble. She was telling me in great detail about the latest adventures of a reality show she watched religiously. A movement behind her caught my attention. I moved to get a better look and saw that Brianna was walking with her catlike gait toward our table. We had decided that she wouldn't talk to me at school. Panicking, I turned quickly to Morgan, hoping Brianna would go away. I plunged desperately into the conversation, hoping that my coldness would discourage her. I laughed nervously. Morgan was looking at me funny.

Brianna arrived at our table, as I had feared.

"Hello! How are you?" Morgan greeted her enthusiastically.

"Very well. Thank you, Morgan."

"Brianna! Come and sit next to me. How are you doing?" Joe asked.

Brianna had barely sat down when my other friends were already greeting her warmly. All the girls turned to her, and a lively and friendly discussion ensued. Perplexed, I joined the conversation, trying to keep my natural demeanor despite the disconcerting situation. This sudden turnaround was upsetting.

Why were the girls suddenly accepting Brianna so willingly?

A far-fetched reason made its way into my mind. What if it was a spell? I had to accept the inconceivable—Brianna was a witch. It was the only plausible conclusion. Nothing else could explain what was unfolding before my eyes. Considering what had happened with Christian, I had to face the obvious.

"What about you, Emily?"

I returned my attention to the conversation. Lost in my thoughts, I had completely lost the thread of the discussion.

"We're going shopping Friday night. Do you want to come with us?" Vanessa asked.

"Why not?" I said without thinking. I was too bewildered to react otherwise.

The bell rang and interrupted the unusual moment. Brianna gave me a knowing wink and left for her first class of the day. She confirmed my suspicions—she had bewitched my friends.

Come to think of it, the situation was amusing. My friends—*possessed*, I chuckled to myself at the thought. Maybe my life would get more interesting now that Brianna could join us and divert the conversation to more interesting topics. It wouldn't hurt to get my friends interested in something other than gossip. A little culture would do them a world of good.

The routine changed drastically for me from that day on. I had a renewed enthusiasm for my social life in particular, which positively affected other aspects of my life. Thanks to Brianna, the popularity rating of our group of friends had skyrocketed. I felt like the queen of the school. We would walk down the hallways arm in arm, laughing effusively. The other students would say hello to us if they dared to address us, while the more self-conscious ones would be silent for fear of being ridiculed.

My friends were very welcoming to Brianna. It seemed like

she had always been part of our group, growing up with us and sharing our childhood games.

* * *

As planned, my friends and I went to the mall together on Friday. We had a great time browsing the stores and trying on some great outfits. I picked up a few items on sale to update my wardrobe. I felt different and wanted to reflect a little more daring in my look.

Not only was Brianna accepted by my friends, but other changes had taken place in our environment. I noticed the teachers were much more tolerant of her. They always accepted her excuses for not completing her assignments on time, even the most outlandish ones. She got good marks on her presentations and essays. For example, I noticed that the English teacher was no longer picking up on her grammatical errors. In physical education class, she was named captain, an honor usually reserved only for the most athletically gifted students.

I felt invincible by Brianna's side. Arm in arm, we walked the halls of our kingdom, greeting our subjects as we went. Everyone would turn and smile at us. They invited us to all the parties. All we had to do was choose from the invitations. The more time passed, the more I enjoyed my new popularity.

I prepared myself to take part in the regional final of the crystal contest. I had just learned that Mr. Thompson, our teacher, selected our crystal to be in the competition along with the crystal grown by Joseph and William.

I was so excited. We were going to travel in a small bus rented for the occasion. We were going to Montreal. Finally—some action. It would be a big change from being stuck in this little, lost town.

On Wednesday evening, I packed my bags with maniacal precision. I didn't want to forget anything. We were leaving on Thursday afternoon, right after school, and I had to be ready. I gathered my toothbrush, a very professional set of clothes for our day at the show on Friday, comfortable shoes for standing all day, and of course, pajamas. I'd chosen the green ones with the smiling bears because they were my warmest and my mother had insisted that it was always too cold in hotel rooms. Never mind if Brianna would make fun of my choice. I had no intention of shivering under the sheets.

Thursday felt like it would never end. I kept glancing at the clock, no matter what class I was in. To pass time, I made an agenda with my dreams, clothes to buy, shops to visit, trips to take... I was distracted, and all I could think about was my weekend in Montreal.

Concentrating on a scribble, I chewed the end of my pencil. The English teacher noticed my distraction and asked me a question to bring my attention back to whatever subject was being discussed. Confused, I stammered.

"Come on, Emily. You're not paying attention," the teacher said. "This information will surely be very useful for the test next week. Is it noted, everyone?"

I sighed quietly. Despite the teacher's obvious clue, I doubted that half of the students had noted what he said in order to be ready for the test. I was disappointed in most of my companions for their lack of intellectual alertness. I wrote the answer and circled it with my neon green highlighter. This test would be as easy as the others.

At last, the last bell of the day rang. With renewed energy, I rushed out of the classroom. I went to my locker to throw my books inside and quickly retrieved my backpack filled to the brim to take with me on the weekend trip. I joined Brianna at the small bus that was waiting for us near the entrance of the school. She was carefully carrying the crystal that we had grown with methodical care. I smiled at her.

"Brianna, watch out for our precious!" I said to tease her, making a gurgling noise with the c in "precious" to imitate Gollum from *Lord of the Rings*.

"Don't worry. He's mine, the precious one," she said, smiling at my reference to one of our favorite movies. She held the crystal close to her heart to show the solemnity of her protection.

"Let's go, my dear friend," I said, putting my hand on her shoulder in a friendly manner.

"Adventure awaits us!" she said as she got on the bus first.

Mr. Thompson was already waiting for us along with Joseph and William, who made up the other team selected to represent the school at the competition. They were sitting on their own benches but were heckling each other. I waved hesitantly and took a seat next to Brianna. Mr. Thompson called out to the driver, "Here we go." The car started.

Brianna and I sat on the hard bus seat and chatted animatedly. Joseph and William took the bench in front of us, turning around and leaning against the backrest to better talk to us.

"Hi, girls," said Joseph in a honeyed voice.

Clearly, he thought he was pleasing us with his seductive skills. Brianna giggled.

"Hi, I'm William," the other boy said, holding out his hand

like we were strangers.

He seemed more at ease, and above all, more natural than his companion. His intense gaze made me look down. He was really sexy. How had I never noticed that about him? But it seemed as though he was noticing me for the first time too.

"Hi," I said at the same time as Brianna in a tone that I wanted to be casual.

During the three hours of the trip, we talked with the two boys. We were gradually discovering their personalities and senses of humor. I felt more comfortable with them by the time the bus finally crossed the bridge into town. I looked out the bus window at the lights. *How lively it is! What a beautiful city!*

I promised myself that I would continue my university studies in Montreal.

The little bus weaved its way through the ever-increasing traffic, and the driver finally dropped us off in front of our downtown hotel. Brianna and I shared a room on the twentieth floor. Excited as a flea to get away from the adults, I grabbed the swipe card handed to me by the teacher and took off like an arrow toward the elevator, guiding Brianna.

"Don't forget to meet us tomorrow morning at seven o'clock sharp in the reception hall. We'll all have breakfast together at the restaurant down here," Mr. Thompson said, pointing to the little bistro.

"Yes, sure!" I said.

The elevator doors were already closing behind us with a small bell-like sound. I pressed button twenty to take us to our room. Laughing, we made our way through the labyrinth of corridors and finally found the door to room 2034. I slid the magnetic card into the mechanism, went inside, and eagerly discovered our new surroundings. I pushed back the curtain to look at the illuminated city.

"Look at the bathroom. Marble everywhere. It's very modern. I love it!"

I spun around to admire the scenery. I put my wheeled suitcase on the first bed. Brianna moved to her bed next to the window.

"Come on. It's just a hotel room," Brianna said. "They all look the same after all."

I hated it when she got all superior. She was ruining a special moment. Pouting, I bitingly retorted, "Maybe for you, the great traveler. I didn't have the chance to travel around the world with my parents."

"Okay, no need to be offended. I didn't mean to break your enthusiasm," she said.

She took her place on her bed like a queen on her throne. She pushed back a lock of red hair that was falling over her eyes. I sighed. That was the only apology I could expect from Brianna. I fell on my back on my bed.

"What do you think of our companions?" Brianna quickly changed the subject, probably to lighten the mood. She seemed determined to lead me down a path I felt was slippery.

She gave me one of her teasing winks, but I had no intention of falling into her trap.

"Mr. Thompson and Joseph? Ah…" I needed to think of a way to get her to drop the subject. I had to give her just enough information to satisfy her curiosity but not enough that she would ask me again.

"They're nice," I said neutrally, hoping she would leave it at that.

That was not knowing her very well.

"Emily, my friend, I've never seen you in such a state," she said. "Except maybe with Christian."

I cringed at the sound of that name.

"I saw how you laughed at all of William's jokes. Come on, admit it!" She threw a pillow at me. I turned to unpack my suitcase and to hide my burning cheeks.

"Your eyes were so bright that you blinded me with all those stars!" She fluttered her eyelashes and laughed.

I didn't think I'd been that transparent. Had William deciphered my behavior? Did he think I was a pathetic girl desperate to meet someone? At the thought, shame overtook me.

Brianna rose to join me, turned me around, and held me still in front of her. Docile, I let her do it, but I refused to meet her eyes and stared at the floor.

She teased me, shaking me like a plum tree. She seemed to be having the time of her life.

"Brianna, I don't want to talk about this right now," I said. "I have to get my clothes ready for tomorrow and practice my presentation one last time."

"Emily, tell me the truth," she said.

I couldn't force her to give up on the subject. "If I tell you I like him, do you promise to leave me alone and not to embarrass me in front of him?"

"Maybe," she said.

"Promise!"

"Well, I promise," she said reluctantly.

"So, yes. I confess, I find him charming. I never even noticed him before today. But after spending the bus ride talking to him, I discovered he has such a distinct personality. When he makes me laugh, I see him with fresh eyes."

"I knew it," she said triumphantly, jumping up and down and pointing at me. "You have a crush on William!"

"You promised! No more talk. Case closed."

I grabbed the remote and turned on the TV in an attempt to change the subject once and for all. "So, what are we watching?" I asked Brianna. "A horror movie?"

"Forget it!" She snatched the remote from my hand and threw it on the bed.

"We're in Montreal, no one's watching us, and you want to watch television." She shook her head in disappointment. "You don't know how to have fun, Emily."

Mischievously, she rushed to her suitcase. She plunged her hand into it and theatrically took out two brightly colored tops—a fuchsia camisole with white lace on the neckline and a black sleeveless sweater with a silver face printed on the front and back. She showed them to me like a toreador waving a flag in front of the eyes of an enraged bull.

"Let's go out, baby! Do you want the pink one or the black one?"

"You've lost your mind!" I said. "We're not going out alone at night in this unknown city. It's not safe."

I sat resolutely on my bed, folding my arms to show my disagreement with her reckless idea.

Brianna didn't seem fazed. "You really need me, poor thing. You'll end up an old maid if you keep going down this road," she said, shaking her head.

"Anyway, we're not even old enough to get into bars," I said. "They'll never let us in. It's a lose-lose situation."

It was as if she had heard nothing.

"Here. I want the black one," she said, throwing me the pink camisole.

It hit me in the face, which made her laugh. She was already putting on the sweater, which went perfectly with her tight jeans. She slipped her long legs into black stiletto boots and zipped them up. Whistling, she took out her makeup box. She was determined to carry out her insane plan.

"Brianna, aren't you listening to me?"

"You're underestimating me again?" she said with another of her winks.

She was exasperating me with her winking.

Looking at herself in the mirror, Brianna expertly drew a long, black line across her eyelids to highlight her green cat eyes.

Her determination made me think. I, who only a few weeks ago had complained that my life was depressing and boring… I was finally getting what I had wished for. Yet, I felt uneasy stepping out of my comfort zone. I wanted to be more adventurous, sure, but going out with Brianna at night in a big city seemed a bit too dangerous.

But I got to thinking that we only have one life to live, right? I would not let this unique opportunity pass me by, no matter how crazy and risky the idea. I put on the camisole, which fit me like a glove. Brianna approached me with her black eye pencil.

"Don't move."

I let her trace the outline of my eyes. Then she reached into her suitcase and handed me a pair of pink, glittery sandals with dizzying heels and *real jewels*. My reflection in the mirror impressed me. I almost looked like a grown-up.

We were laughing like crazy as we left the hotel. Brianna hailed a cab like a pro and gave the driver the address.

"Do you know the bars here?" I asked her, incredulous.

"You won't believe your eyes, Emily. My cousin recommended this club to me. According to him, it's the place to be on Thursday nights. All the most popular college boys from around the area meet there."

I was very excited at the prospect. I could hardly wait while I sat in the back seat of the taxi. But when the car pulled up in front of the club, my excitement deflated. The line was around the block. Brianna paid the fare. I moved to the end of the line with my head down, but she started to pull me straight to the front where the doorman guarded the entrance.

"Come on!" she said to rush me.

He was the stereotypical doorman, with a hulking build and muscles that would make many a football player envious. He wore a leather jacket and dark glasses. Brianna didn't even look at him and ran for the door. Quickly, he blocked her entrance with his enormous arms. Clearly, he was a regular at the gym. I blinked at the thought of the trouble Brianna was about to get us into.

"Hey, you!" the doorman said. "Where are you going?"

"We come here every Thursday, and you still don't recognize me? Look at your list, big guy," she said in the most condescending tone I'd ever heard. "Brianna Ducharme."

The doorman grunted. He was obviously not happy to be spoken to in that tone, especially by a frail girl like Brianna. The voice she used to speak to him made me fear for our safety. The man lowered his sunglasses to stare at her with his menacing brown eyes. She held his gaze and insisted on pointing to his list. He grudgingly ran his finger down the names. To my surprise, it stopped on a name.

"Come in," he said, obviously confused.

I followed Brianna into the club. I couldn't believe it. We

were in. "How did you get your name on the VIP list?"

"It wasn't there," she said.

"What do you mean?"

"I fogged his mind," she said, sweeping the air with her hand as if it were a negligible fact.

But what was she talking about? I was still discovering new powers in her, which was worrying. But it was useless to question her here and now. The music was playing loudly, so it would be hard for her to hear me. I promised myself that I would talk to her again at the first opportunity.

Brianna was already heading for the bar. Panicked, I stopped her. "Are you insane? We're not even allowed to be here, and you want to order booze?"

"Relax, I don't like beer, or alcohol, for that matter. I prefer a good energy drink."

Relieved, I took out my wallet. "All right. I'll buy."

At the bar, I ordered two drinks, which the server gave us in glasses filled with ice. I handed Brianna her glass, and she clinked it against mine.

"Cheers," she said.

Leaning against the counter, I took my first sip of the delicious, icy liquid. The place was packed with handsome guys. I didn't know which way to turn. I caught a few of them looking at me, which made me extremely happy. Brianna knew how to pick out clothes for a night on the town. A tall, dark, and handsome guy smiled at me. I smiled back, surprised at my boldness.

With our drinks in hand, Brianna led me onto the dance floor. Smiling, we made our way through the crowd of dancers. The deafening music electrified us. My friend showed me her best moves, and we had a lot of fun.

The man with the beautiful smile approached us. I was trembling with nervousness. Brianna winked at me. He came a little closer and started dancing with us. He put his mouth to my ear to talk to me and told me his name was Thomas. A shiver of pleasure ran down my spine. Brianna wasn't left to herself either. A handsome guy had approached her too.

I spent a magical evening with Thomas. He made me laugh, and I didn't notice the time pass. I danced the last slow dance in his arms and buried my nose in his neck. He smelled so good. I closed my eyes to savor the moment. He placed a kiss on my lips. Suddenly, light dazzled me. It was the signal that the bar was about to close. Brianna grabbed my wrist and pulled me toward the exit. I made an attempt to say goodbye to my Prince Charming, but we were already out the door.

"Hey! He wanted me to leave him my number."

"Forget it," Brianna said. "Long-distance love is hell."

We got into the first available taxi. It was after three in the morning. I had been dancing and laughing all night, and my ears were ringing. *What an unforgettable evening!* When we arrived at our room without incident, the fatigue caught up with us. I sighed with relief when I could finally remove the dizzying shoes that were torturing my feet. Exhausted, I collapsed into bed.

A few hours later, the shrill sound of the alarm clock assaulted my eardrums, and I woke up with a start. What an ordeal. I rushed to stop it. I felt as if I had not slept at all. Four hours of sleep were definitely not enough for me, but it was the day of the exhibition. Sitting on the edge of the bed, with hair flying in all directions from dried hairspray and makeup smearing my face, I groaned.

I got up to go to the bathroom, grumbling. A look into our

bathroom mirror at my face filled me with horror.

"Brianna," I said.

My complexion was scary pale, and my bloodshot eyes featured dark circles under them. I was scaring myself. I needed a good shower and a big cup of coffee, although I hated the bitter taste of the beverage.

"I'm coming," she said, still half-asleep.

She walked to the doorway of the bathroom and tossed me a small, candy-pink bag full of stuff without even looking at me. I barely caught it and opened it to discover its contents—foundation, eyeshadow, concealer, eye drops, and more.

"You really had it all figured out," I said with admiration.

This girl kept surprising me. I hurried to the shower. Once I got rid of the sweat from our evening, I felt more awake. I put on the concealer and foundation, spreading a thick layer over my face. I put drops in my eyes to reduce the redness. Satisfied, I left the bathroom, wrapped in a thick, white towel, to make room for Brianna.

"Last evening will remain our secret," Brianna said, rushing into the bathroom.

I put on my outfit for the presentation—a black skirt and an immaculate white shirt. I tied my hair up in a low bun at the nape of my neck, completing my professional look. Teasingly, I winked at myself in the mirror.

"Hurry, we'll be late," I called to Brianna.

We were to meet Mr. Thompson, Joseph, and William for breakfast at seven o'clock. Brianna hurriedly got dressed. She had done her makeup expertly and transformed herself into a model student in just a few minutes. We were going to impress the judges today, I was sure. Brianna carefully lifted our precious crystal and brought it with her.

As I stepped out of the elevator at the appointed time, I spotted Mr. Thompson, Joseph, and William waiting for us in the lobby.

"Come on. I'm starving," our teacher said with a friendly smile. "The restaurant is right here."

"I'm hungry too. It's like I've been dancing all night," Brianna said with a mischievous smile.

I looked down so that my amused expression would not betray me.

We sat down at a table by the large bay window. I ordered my classic two eggs and bacon for breakfast, but this time I added coffee to ward off sleep. Fortunately, there weren't many customers, and the service was quick. I devoured my breakfast with a healthy appetite. All the activity of the night before had made me hungry.

After the last bite, I wiped my mouth with the cloth napkin. It was time to get down to business. We were here to win a contest. Mr. Thompson settled the bill.

The showroom was at the back of the hotel. Brianna was carrying our crystal. I quickly spotted a banner with our names floating above one table. She carefully placed the jar containing our crystal on the white cotton tablecloth. All that remained was to welcome the curious visitors, but especially the judges, who circulated incognito among the crowd. With the morning's adrenaline rush over, I was having trouble keeping my eyes open despite the coffee I'd grimaced over. My ears were still ringing, and blisters covered my feet because of Brianna's high heels. I wasn't in the best of moods to represent my school with a smile all day.

Brianna left for a few moments and brought us more strong coffee. Since I rarely drank coffee, it didn't take long for the caffeine to kick in and for me to finally feel wide awake. I smiled and explained our project to our visitors.

By the end of the day, I was completely exhausted. I had given my all in order to do our team and our school proud. The visitors had left the room. Suddenly, a voice came over the microphone. "We ask every team to get closer to the stage."

Brianna gave me a pat on the back for a job well done. To my relief, the day had gone well. In a few hours, we would be back on the bus that would take us home.

On the stage, a tri-level podium had been set up for the unveiling of the winners, and a man was speaking into a microphone. "Congratulations to all the selected teams. If you are here today, you are already winners. Now it's time to announce the names of this year's top performers."

There was silence in the room.

"I remind you that the judges evaluated the crystals on size, shape, edges, faces, clarity, and opacity. Your presentation to the visitors also influenced your score." The man turned to a woman in the crowd. "Diane?"

A woman in a black suit took over the microphone. She had a paper in her hands. "Thank you, John. For this year's edition of the Larger than Life Crystal contest, third place goes to…"

My heart stopped beating.

"Nicolas Patterson and Jessica Hernandez from Martensville High School!"

The crowd applauded the winners, who proudly took their place on the third step of the podium.

"Second place goes to…"

I held my breath.

"Brianna Ducharme and Emily Reed from Frankville High School!"

Great! I jumped into Brianna's arms. We stood on the second step of the podium. Not being very good at sports, I never imagined I would step on a podium in my life. I heard nothing that was said afterward, not even who had taken first place. I picked up our trophy and held it up. *We got second place!*

When the awards ceremony was over, it was with regret that I had to step down from the podium. Mr. Thompson came to join us. He seemed thrilled with our second place. Joseph and William also congratulated us, even though I could see that they were a little jealous of our victory.

What a great experience! How beautiful life is!

Chapter 6

The following week, Brianna and I arrived at school triumphant, trophy in hand. Sitting at our table, the girls congratulated us on our second-place finish. I felt happy. As promised, Brianna and I didn't say a word about our trip to the club. It was our secret.

Suddenly, I felt the atmosphere at the table change. Turning around to see what Morgan was looking at so intently, I saw Lucy heading straight for Brianna and me. A wave of panic and hope swept over the girls.

Lucy was a senior. She had long, silky golden hair that cascaded over her shoulders. She was in the most popular band in school and would surely win the crown at the prom. Just seeing her approach, my heart stopped beating. She was holding two red envelopes in her hand. I was breathless. Were they invitations to her famous annual Christmas party? The party was legendary. We talked about it for weeks.

Fortunately, she soon came close to us, for I was in a state. My body could not stand the intense suspense. She greeted us and handed an envelope to Brianna. The second one was for me.

"I hope you girls can come. It will be fun." she said and walked away.

The envelope was shaking in my hands. I was in shock and couldn't believe my luck. I held back a victorious cry in my throat. It was the happiest day of my life. Caroline snatched the envelope from my hands, took out the invitation, and admired it with envy. The promise of the golden letters shimmered on a fiery-red card. Caroline recited aloud, for the benefit of all.

Party by invitation only

You are invited to the party of the year! Come to my house on Saturday, October 19, to celebrate my birthday. Show up in your best clothes, starting at nine p.m.

Lucy

I was willing to bet that Brianna and I were the only eleventh-graders invited to the party of the year. The girls were boiling with envy. Brianna had a smile on her face. A triumphant smile.

Like a bolt of lightning, a brilliant idea flashed through my mind. Christian had to hear the news. He would bite his fingers off for rejecting me, now that I was popular and at the very top of the school food chain. It was too late for him. He'd lost his chance. No way was I going to fall back into his arms. I still had my pride.

I had my Spanish class with Christian in a few moments. All I had to do was bring the envelope and place it on my desk for Christian to see.

That was exactly what I did.

With the red envelope in plain view, I watched for his reaction out of the corner of my eye. When his gaze finally fell on the invitation, I noticed disbelief and then jealousy in his eyes. An intense feeling of satisfaction washed over me. He knew what the envelope represented. I gloated inwardly while keeping a straight face. Christian tried to get my attention, but I ignored him with relish. Anyway, Spanish class was starting.

I heard barely anything of Mr. Martinez's teaching during the class. All I could think about was the party that was fast approaching. For the occasion, I needed to go all out with my outfit. There was even time for me to get my hair fixed at my hairdresser. The best looks for the occasion flashed through my mind, and I analyzed them one by one. Brianna would surely agree to come with me to the mall this week to find the best clothing. Pictures from the party would be all over the Internet, and some would probably be in the yearbook. The ultimate accolade would be to be in the book.

This invitation had been unexpected. Brianna had never caught Lucy's eye, and now Lucy was inviting her to the party of the year. A doubt popped into my mind, but I had no desire to dwell on it. I shook it off with the back of my hand. Why waste this moment of pure bliss on trifles? I was finally going to rise to the top of the school's social ladder, and there was no way my conscience was going to spoil the opportunity.

As soon as the bell rang, I rushed out of class to get to Brianna. I avoided Christian's questions as I passed him in the hall. I had no desire to talk to him. I was savoring my revenge, and he meant nothing to me. When that thought crossed my mind, I felt a twinge of regret and knew it wasn't true. But I had to hold on to that lie to ease the intense pain of his rejection.

In the hallway, I ran into William.

"Hi, crystal pro!" he said.

His jeans fit him so well, I blushed. He was very classy for a teenager, with his Lacoste polo shirt and his trendy sneakers. I couldn't believe it had taken me so long to notice him.

"Hi," I said, trying to control the blood that was rushing to my cheeks.

Alas, I felt myself blushing even more and looked away to hide my reaction.

He leaned casually against the wall, signaling he was in the mood for conversation. "So, what did you do with your medal?"

"It's somewhere in my room," I said, lying.

Our trophy was displayed at school, but Brianna and I had also gotten medals. I had proudly showed mine to my parents as soon as I got back from Montreal. They were very proud, and my mother had jumped for joy. My father had hung the medal in the kitchen for all to see. But I had no intention of bragging about it to William. Pretentious students are not very popular.

William's eyes rested on the red envelope on top of my notebook. His beautiful blue eyes rounded.

"Wow. An invitation to Lucy's party." He whistled. His eyes were admiring.

I felt myself blush once more under his gaze, but I took a deep breath to calm my panicked heart.

"I didn't know you were friends," William said.

Honestly, neither did I. But I owed this invitation to Brianna. Embarrassed and wanting to avoid more questions, I cut the conversation short. "That's right. Brianna is waiting for me. See you."

William seemed disappointed when I left him, but I didn't intend to linger and answer more questions on the subject. *Whew!* That had been a narrow escape.

Brianna was waiting for me, leaning against my locker. I was relieved that it was the end of the day. I couldn't concentrate anymore. She took my arm and pulled me toward the exit. I saw Caroline and Ashley out of the corner of my eye. They looked surprised and jealous. They were talking behind my back. I could feel it, but I didn't care. I was at the top now, and I had no intention of pretending to be interested in them anymore. They bored me to death, and I didn't have to worry about them anymore. What a relief.

"So, are you ready for glory?" Brianna asked, a roguish smile on her face.

"I can hardly believe it! I've been waiting for this."

We left the school together, and each of us went home.

When my mother arrived from work, she noticed my smile right away.

"You're in a good mood. What happened at school today?" she asked, hanging up her coat.

I was already overwhelmed, so I threw my school bag on the bench and jumped up and down. "I'm invited to Lucy's birthday party on Saturday! It's *the* party of the year. All the most popular students will be there. Can I go?" I said, begging.

"Let me think about it," she said, putting a finger on her chin. "Sure, you can go."

I shouted as I jumped into the air.

"I trust you, but you have to keep earning it. I don't want you to use alcohol. And certainly not drugs. Do you understand me?"

I threw my arms around her neck to thank her.

I was floating on cloud nine at the thought of being accepted by the students in the school's most prominent circle. My cell phone vibrated in my jeans pocket. I had just received a text from Brianna.

What are you wearing to the party? she asked

I have nothing to wear.

Let's go shopping Friday after school.
Okay.

As planned, Brianna and I headed to the mall on Friday. We dedicated our entire evening to finding the perfect outfit for the event. After going to my three favorite stores and not finding anything suitable, I felt my stress level spike. What if I couldn't find anything? I would probably make a fool of myself and ruin my chances of getting with the in crowd permanently. Brianna did not seem to be discouraged. She was still in a good mood and seemed to be enjoying every moment.

She walked purposefully to another shop. It was the CarSo shop, where the trendiest students got their clothes. I'd been there once before, but the prices were so high that I had come away empty-handed.

Brianna selected pieces as she scrolled down the rows of clothing. She threw them into my arms, smiling, without even looking at the tags. Then we headed to the fitting rooms. She found a dress in the lot and handed it to me.

"Here, this dress is perfect for you," she said.

It was formfitting, with a V-neck. The fabric was black and silky. Two red stripes outlined the waist, making the look even more flamboyant. I pulled back the curtain and slipped the dress on, then I stepped out of the little booth and stood in front of the mirror. The reflection left me speechless. I had finally found the perfect outfit. My stomach tightened. How much was this little gem going to cost me?

Brianna came out of the cabin and let out a giggle of delight when she saw me. She swung me around to assess her choice. "I knew this dress would look great on you! It's just like you."

She rushed to the accessory rack and handed me a long necklace made of silver rings and red beads along with a matching bracelet. She completed the ensemble with a pair of red sandals. I tied the thin leather straps to my ankles. All the pieces worked together beautifully. I dared not look at the prices.

I waited for Brianna to finish her fitting. She, too, found a dress for the evening. As I admired her style, I noticed she knew how to show off her body. The green of the outfit brought out the shine in her beautiful red hair, and she completed her look with jewelry and shoes. She was stunning. She also bought a sweater and a pair of jeans to add to her wardrobe.

I was dreading paying at the cash register. I swallowed hard when I saw that my bill came to $367.86. That was almost my entire savings. I paid the bill and tried to justify the purchase to myself. I was investing in my future, after all. Popularity was of paramount importance. My logic was weak, but I deliberately ignored my doubts. I pushed them into the furthest corner of my brain. I was going to turn every head at the party.

I didn't want my mom to see my bag from CarSo. She knew that the store was expensive, and she definitely wouldn't approve of spending so much money on one outfit. When I got home, I took the clothes out of the bag, hastily removed all the tags, and stuffed them into the empty bag. I buried the bag in the outside garbage can, well hidden under the trash. I put the clothes into another bag.

"Emily, is that you?" my mother asked as I walked through the door.

"Come and see what I've found," I said excitedly. "A dress for Lucy's birthday party!"

My mother turned her attention from her laptop to admire my acquisition. "Wow, Emily. Put it on. I want to see your new look."

My mother understood that this party was very important to me. I hurriedly put on the dress, adjusted the accessories, and showed her the final take by spinning around. A radiant smile lit up her face.

"You've become a woman, Emily," she said. "You look great. I'm sure Christian will kick himself for not wanting to date you."

"He's not even invited." I said, triumphantly. "And he was green with envy when he saw my invitation, which I had strategically placed for him to see."

I laughed loudly, and my mother laughed with me. At that very moment, I realized I was finally happy.

The day of the long-awaited party finally arrived. We planned to get ready at Brianna's house, and her aunt would drive us to the party and pick us up. I was to sleep at Brianna's and not walk home until the next morning.

I arrived at Brianna's house with what I called "my war material." We were excited about the great night ahead of us. I had butterflies in my stomach. I put on my makeup while Brianna curled her long red hair.

After hours of perfuming, creaming, applying makeup, and styling, we were finally ready to go on the attack. I couldn't admit it to myself, but I thought I was beautiful.

I complimented Brianna. "You look amazing! You should be a stylist. You have an innate talent."

We went down to the kitchen. Brianna's aunt was waiting for us, sipping herbal tea and leafing through a magazine. She looked up at us. She was delighted and applauded us. "What beautiful women. Ready for the party?"

"Oh, yes!"

We piled into Brianna's aunt's compact economy car. During

the drive, I felt feverish, and my hands were sweaty. Finally, the car pulled up in front of Lucy's impressive home, a large Victorian-style house made of gray stone with several turrets on top. It looked like a castle. The party was already in full swing. All the lights in the house were on. Lucy's parents had given her free rein tonight.

I got out of the car and tried to look as casual as possible in my tight dress. Since I wasn't used to heels, I grabbed Brianna by the arm to steady myself and to balance on my stilts.

"Brianna, there's no way you're letting me down tonight. We're staying together."

"Don't worry. You'll be fine. You'll be the first to let me down and make new friends." She smiled at me and gave me her usual wink. We were going to be the queens of the party.

As soon as we walked through the door, the music filled our ears. Lucy's parents had hired a DJ for the evening. Several people surrounded the party girl. I didn't recognize them all. Some boys were older and very attractive. I was intimidated, but I didn't want to let it show. Brianna went straight to Lucy and kissed her, as if they were old friends.

"Lucy! How beautiful you look tonight," Brianna said. "Thank you for inviting us."

"Brianna, I'm so glad you're here. You are beautiful! Let me introduce you to Bruno, John, Gabriel, Hannah, Riley, and of course, you already know my best friend, Haley."

"Hi, everyone," Brianna said.

She turned to John, a very sexy young man. I estimated him to be nineteen or twenty. She confidently held out a hand. "John, I'm Brianna. How did you meet Lucy?"

Brianna pushed her curly hair back and gave John a seductive look. John did not seem indifferent to her approach. I was impressed. I was going to have to pull out all the stops too. Chasing away my shyness, I stepped out of Brianna's shadow and addressed Riley after greeting Lucy. The music was deafening. I yelled to make myself understood.

"So, Riley, how is college?"

"I'm studying communication, which is very interesting," Riley said. "Unfortunately, I still have a lot of mandatory courses to take, and I can't wait to finish them and finally move on to my major. Because the courses in my field are fascinating. What about you?"

"Oh, me? The sooner I finish high school, the better. I need a change of scenery."

"And what will you do after you graduate?"

"I don't know yet. As long as it's far from here. I was in Montreal last week, and I liked it. Maybe I would like to study there."

He smiled at me. I was doing well after all. Riley's interest pushed me to keep going.

"But first, I want to spend some time outside the country to explore new horizons," I said.

"You want to dance?"

Riley took my hand and led me deeper into the living room. Dozens of students were moving to the rhythm of the music. Some couples were embracing. I would have loved to be in the place of one of those girls. For example, that beautiful blonde sitting on her lover's lap, kissing him full on the lips. I thought that I would like Christian and me to be like that. An angry shiver ran down my spine at the thought of him.

Astonished, I shook my head to come to my senses. I was in the presence of a college boy, who was listening to me and wanted to dance with me. There was no reason to feel sorry for myself. Smiling at Riley, I let the rhythm take over my body.

I felt great. I loved the way dancing made me feel. My hips were moving in perfect harmony with the rhythm. I could see that Riley was trying to get closer to me. I let him put his hands on my waist. When they slid down to my buttocks, I stepped back. It was too fast for me. He didn't insist and left. Probably looking for a more collaborative prey. I preferred to dance a little more. A few boys approached me, but none really interested me. I was still polite, making conversation and laughing at their jokes.

Later, Brianna came to join me on the dance floor for a few dance steps. But it was already getting late. Fortunately, the evening had gone off without a hitch. I could even say that I had a great time. I'd had all that stress for nothing.

Brianna's aunt came to pick us up around one in the morning. In Brianna's room, I had put my sleeping bag on the floor. Without removing our makeup, without even brushing our teeth, we went to bed. We were exhausted. Still, I couldn't sleep.

"Brianna, did you see that guy I was dancing with? Riley? He was great. He goes to college. Can you believe that? And he danced with me."

"I knew you liked him," Brianna said. "And what do you say about my Apollo?"

We spent part of the night reminiscing about the best moments and telling each other about the gossip we'd heard during the evening.

When I got home the next morning, I had a smile on my face, and my eyes were more rimmed than ever. I couldn't remember ever feeling this good. I was partying with the popular kids now. My life had changed so much in such a short time. It was unexpected. Finally, I felt loved and accepted.

An uncomfortable thought kept creeping into my mind. Was this sudden popularity because of Brianna's magic? A terrible doubt nagged at me.

I'd been skeptical of her powers at first, but after what happened with Christian… Besides, she was making friends with everyone now, even the teachers. She could show up late and forget her homework, and none of them would punish her. Would Brianna know how to draw an acceptable line on her magic? Come to think of it, any manipulation was unnatural and, therefore, morally reprehensible. She had already crossed the line. She simply should not have used her witchcraft for the purposes she had.

By taking advantage of the situation, I was guilty by association. I was getting everything I had ever dreamed of—an interesting life, a kick-ass best friend, and a pass into the inner circles of popular society. However, getting those things dishonestly left a bitter taste in my mouth.

I shook my head to get rid of the depressing thoughts.

"There's no such thing as magic," I said to myself.

That afternoon, pictures of the party were already flooding my Facebook account. I was tagged in some pictures, along with Brianna and Riley. Fortunately, I was photogenic. I had received several friend requests lately and even more today. I didn't dare say no to anyone, even though the requests were sometimes from acquaintances I'd run into in the halls of the school. The number of my virtual *friends* kept growing.

On Monday, Brianna and I arrived at the lunch table triumphantly. My friends had seen the pictures of the party on Facebook, and they seemed green with envy, especially Morgan and Caroline. I thought they would want to know everything about the party. Instead, they avoided the subject with surgical precision. Brianna saw through their game as clearly as I did and made fun of them. She winked at me.

"What a night!" Brianna said. "It was not to be missed. Was it, Emily?"

She didn't even wait for my answer and went on. "A choice selection of males. I didn't know what to do. Have you seen my picture with Carl?"

Once again, she continued without delay. "We can't wait for next year to relive this memorable moment!"

Dear Brianna, always ready to irritate the shallow crowd. The girls pretended to ignore her and continued their conversation. I laughed under my breath. They could decide to kick us out of their circle, but I didn't care anymore now that I had Brianna.

At noon, I stood in line in the cafeteria, as I had not brought my lunch. The promising menu, a choice of poutine or spaghetti and meat, was still attracting a crowd. The line of students was getting even longer than usual. A little ahead of me, William was also waiting in line.

He turned around and saw me. "Emily! Come on."

Cutting the line in front of a few students, I moved forward, ignoring their disapproving grumbles. "Hi, William. How are you?"

"Cool, cool. So, the party? Was it worth the trip?"

"Oh yes. The party of the year! There were so many people and a DJ. Brianna and I had a great time."

"So, uh… you got any plans Thursday night?" He rubbed his neck uncomfortably.

As a result, my cheeks turned red. "Um, no. Nothing special. No," I said.

"Ah uh, how about a movie?"

"Why not?"

Relieved, I felt the tension ease between us. A shiver ran down my spine. I liked William. He was cute and, above all, intelligent.

"Okay, cool," he said, smiling shyly. "So, I'll come by your place around seven next Thursday?"

"Yes. Okay."

We had already arrived at the cafeteria door. I grabbed the first available plate of spaghetti and paid at the cash register. Turning back, I waved to William, who went off to join his friends. I was on cloud nine. *William is interested in me!*

I headed for our usual table. Brianna wasn't there. She had warned me she had to meet with a teacher to retake an exam she had failed. The girls were already deep in conversation. With my plate full of pasta dripping with tomato sauce in front of me, I was absentmindedly taking part in the girls' superficial conversation. I didn't even want to tell them what had just happened. That was how little I cared about our relationship anymore. Morgan would surely have found something negative to say about William out of simple jealousy. That was what she had done to Caroline when Albert had invited her out. I was dying to tell Brianna everything.

Suddenly, a scream rang out close to our table. I turned around just in time to be hit in the face with a meatball. A food fight. *Awesome!* I picked up my spaghetti with my hands and threw it without even looking at the next table. Tomato pasta hit a younger boy and made a weird stain on his striped shirt. The boy, taken by surprise, laughed as he continued to throw his meatballs methodically, one by one.

All the students were having a great time. The pasta of the day and poutine were flying everywhere, creating disasters on the floor, tables, walls, and clothes. There was a lot of laughter. A panicked supervisor slipped on the red sauce and fell to the floor screaming. I threw the last of my meatballs at my neighbors. The second supervisor, still on her feet, didn't know what to do to stop the madness of over a hundred students and was waving her arms around, shouting, "Enough! Stop it!"

With our plates cleared, there was nothing left to throw, and the action died down on its own. My cheeks were cramping from laughing so hard. I was a mess, but it was worth it. The first food fight in several years had just taken place. It was a memorable moment that would have a place of honor in the yearbook. Just then, a photographer from the newspaper was taking a lot of pictures. I thought of Brianna, who had missed it all. I couldn't wait to tell her all about it. She would be disappointed to have missed this fabulous event.

With a smile on my face, I headed to the bathroom to do my best to erase the marks the fight had left on my appearance. No such luck. The place was crowded with girls who needed to freshen up, just like me. The entire space was occupied. I didn't feel like waiting with the sauce dripping on my face, so I went to the science room to wash up. There were sinks, and I could wash the food off in peace.

I made my way to the room, climbing the steps two at a time. As I had hoped, the door was unlocked. At the sink, I washed my face and rinsed my hair. As I was toweling off my mane, I heard noises coming from the adjoining room, where the ingredients and equipment were stored. I hadn't seen Mr. Thompson, though, so I walked closer. My ear glued to the door, I heard a high-pitched laugh—a female laugh. Intrigued, I stood up on my toes and peeked through the small frosted window of the office.

I stepped back abruptly and hit a desk behind me.

Mr. Thompson was shirtless and kissing someone on the neck. With my hand over my beating heart, I approached the window again. My curiosity was greater than my shock. Discreetly, I looked again. I recognized with horror the smiling face of the woman, who was lying on the desk with Mr. Thompson above her. It was not his wife.

It was Brianna.

Chapter 7

In shock, I rushed out of the classroom, horrified by the sight. I didn't want to be discovered by Brianna. I ran like hell, down the stairs and away from the classroom as fast as I could.

I couldn't believe what I had just seen in that room. Mr. Thompson cheating on his wife with Brianna. What had she done? How could she destroy his family with no shame?

Leaning against a wall, I was having trouble catching my breath. I stood in the deserted cafeteria, my hand on my chest, which was heaving from my exertion. Only an unmotivated janitor was working to pick up the crumpled remains of the battle and restore some order. Awful questions tortured my mind, swirling and threatening. How powerful was Brianna's magic? Where would it end? She was influencing and directing those around her, including me, with no qualms. What if her powers of manipulation were infinite? Was there even a limit?

What about me? Had she cast a spell to make me her puppet?

I gagged. With my hand over my mouth, I rushed to the bathroom. My stomach was churning, and I hoped to make it in time. I hastily pushed open the door to a stall and threw up the few mouthfuls of my dinner. My stomach emptied, and I still had painful spasms. Despite my disgust, I slid to the cold, wet tile floor. My face pressed into my hands, my head full of questions, I sat for a moment, hoping to regain my senses.

The bell announcing the start of afternoon classes rang. As if I were outside my body, I witnessed myself get up. I washed my hands like a robot. My face, tinged with green, reflected in the mirror. I looked terrible. I splashed myself with water, still feeling floaty. Finally, I retrieved my books from my locker and shuffled to my classroom.

The afternoon went by without me. I was present in body but not in spirit. All I could see was Brianna's evil, smiling face as she lay on my teacher's desk.

Finally, the day ended, and I could leave the school. I walked home. I did not hurry. The weak rays of the autumn sun tried to warm me, but I still felt cold. I tried to put my thoughts in order. I pushed open the door of the house.

"Emily!" My mother called. "I finished early today. I'm glad to see you."

"Hello, Mom," I said without enthusiasm.

I sat on a stool in the kitchen. My mother was making lasagna for dinner.

"What's on your mind, baby? I can tell something's up. You seem distant lately."

At that moment, I knew I needed to confide in her, to free myself of this weight that was oppressing my chest. Doubt was gnawing at my mind, and I didn't know what to do. Events were beyond my expertise. Of course, I couldn't tell her everything. My mother would think I was out of my mind if she heard me ranting about Brianna's magical powers. There had to be a way to tell her about my problem without telling her too much.

I sighed. "Mom, I don't know what to do anymore. Brianna… Brianna does things I don't approve of."

"Is she taking drugs? Emily, tell me it's not drugs!" She put down her wooden spoon and looked me straight in the eye, both worried and angry. Drops of sauce splashed into the workspace.

"No, Mom. Don't worry about drugs. Brianna's not interested in them. She's staying away from all that stuff, and you know I am too. It's just that… I don't know how to say it… I saw her with a teacher…"

"Speak up, my dear. I can't hear what you're saying."

"She slept with a teacher! He's married!"

My revelation horrified my mother. She raised her hand to her throat, her eyes bulging.

"Oh my God," she said. She was obviously shocked. "Emily, I don't know how to react. I didn't think such a thing was possible. How can a teacher be so irresponsible?"

"Mom, this isn't—"

Suddenly, as if moved by a spring, she abandoned the stove. "I'm going to call the school principal right now."

She grabbed the cordless phone and headed for her tablet to look up the school's number on the Internet, but I stopped her short by yelling, "No. It's not Mr. Thompson's fault! It's Brianna's. She manipulates everyone around her."

I angrily snatched the handset from her.

"Emily, your teacher's behavior is not tolerable. It's his duty to maintain impeccable behavior with the students. Brianna didn't pull a gun on him. I can't let such an incident go."

She tried to get the phone back. I dodged her.

"I will not testify." I ostensibly crossed my arms over my chest. "I'll say you imagined it, and I said nothing like that."

My mother did not seem at all impressed. Seeing that I would get nowhere with my threats, I relented and tried another approach.

"Mom, I beg you. Don't call the school. Don't tell anyone what I just told you. Swear!" I punctuated my statement with a palm strike on the counter. My reaction surprised my mother. I calmed down a bit.

"I understand you don't agree, but you have to trust me," I said. "I know this is all Brianna's fault. There's no need to ruin Mr. Thompson and his wife's lives. Some things are better left unsaid."

My mother assessed me. I crossed my fingers that I had convinced her.

"Okay, Emily," my mother said and sighed. "I won't interfere in this matter. What do you want from me then? I don't know how to help you."

"Forget what I said, Mom. I can take care of myself." I leapt off the stool, which whirred as it slid across the kitchen tiles.

"But, Emily, wait!"

"Forget it," I said. Flustered, I rushed down the steps to the basement and locked myself in my room. I put my headphones over my ears. I hoped my mother would leave me alone because I needed to think. This situation was more complicated than ever. I was pacing like a caged lion. *Think, think, think.*

What information did I have? I knew Brianna was using magic to get what she wanted. How could I control her? A flash went through my mind. Obviously, I had to learn more about her rituals. I had to know my enemy and her methods in great detail.

I rushed to my laptop and made myself comfortable on my bed, arranging the pillows behind my back. My mind was calming down now that I had a plan. I opened the page of my favorite search engine. I typed in *magic incantation*. A million pages came up. There was so much information. Soporific definitions, incantations, magic with stones, the power of plants, the influence of colors… I didn't know where to turn. I decided to read as much as I could, one page at a time.

With determination, I skimmed through the texts and lingered on the most interesting passages. There were many spells and love potions. Most of them were completely outlandish. Many of the sites lacked credibility, and there was no way of knowing which of the spells Brianna had used on Mr. Thompson. I didn't even know if the spell was among them. So how would I find an antidote?

I rubbed my temples. I could feel a throbbing headache pounding its way through my skull. After scrolling through several pages, a wave of discouragement came over me. So I changed the angle of my search. I typed *witchcraft in the 21st century* into my browser. Once again, I skimmed through the texts. I came across several absurd stories. A woman who was on trial for witchcraft in Africa. A baby who cried incessantly, whose mother thought he was possessed. A kid who talked to the dead. Lineages of women who spread terror around them. One word caught my attention and exploded in my brain—Ducharme. Brianna's last name.

I read the following paragraphs with great attention. The family tree of the Ducharme family went back to the Middle Ages, after which the trail was lost. Inexplicable events were attributed to the Ducharmes. Some women in the family had been executed in Salem during the witch hunts. I fell back on my pillows, hands on my head, stunned.

"Oh, my gosh. I can't believe it. Brianna comes from an impressive line of witches!"

I spent the rest of the evening looking for more information about her family. I discovered that the Ducharme women who gave birth to witches gave them their family name instead of their husband's name. Not very convenient when hiding from witch hunters. I guess they had other ways to disguise themselves.

Time flew by. My reading absorbed all my focus. My mother knocked. I invited her in. She opened the door and leaned against the frame.

"Emily, are you still up? Come on. It's time to go to sleep. You have to rest for your classes tomorrow."

"Do you promise you won't tell anyone about what I told you?"

"I promise. I won't get involved in this."

Reassured, I reluctantly turned off my laptop and placed it on my bedside table. I was on to something, but I was really sleepy. I probably would not find a solution tonight anyway. My eyelids were too heavy, and my concentration was waning.

"I'll put on my pajamas and go to bed right away. Good night, Mom."

My mother said good night and closed the door. I slipped into my pajamas and between the cool white cotton blankets. It had been an exhausting day, and I had no trouble falling asleep.

It's said that sleeping on a problem can help. That was the case for me.

As soon as I opened my eyes, a flash of genius struck my mind. I had to find someone who could find their way through all this information, through the world of magic. A teacher, a mentor who could guide me and show me the way. Only then would I discover how to stop Brianna's schemes.

Enthusiastically, I turned to my laptop again and turned it on. I was impatient, and the machine seemed to take longer than usual to turn on. I would finally find someone who could help me.

It only took me a few minutes of searching to locate Destiny LaGrande's ad. On her divination blog, she described herself as a psychic specializing in nature's interpretation. What did that mean? Was she reading tea leaves? I laughed at the thought. Since she lived nearby, on a secluded street, I contacted her to begin my research.

I clicked on the contact page. When I saw her picture, I realized I had heard of her before. My cousin had gone to see her once, and Destiny had blown her mind with her words. Since that day, my cousin believed in supernatural powers, for which she had fallen a little in my esteem. Since I hadn't believed in that kind of thing myself, I really hadn't paid attention when she told me about it. Now, things were different. I hoped that Destiny could help me.

It was only Tuesday. Four more days of school before the weekend. It was inevitable that I would run into Brianna. It would be impossible for me to avoid her the whole time. I had to act normal, pretend I hadn't seen her on that desk, in that room, in Mr. Thompson's arms. Ugh. A vile shiver ran down my spine at the thought. I shook my head to get the disturbing images out of my mind.

I had to hide my knowledge, though, because I was not at all ready to confront Brianna and her actions. I hoped I could. It was in my best interest to deal with this problem as soon as possible. I had to act soon to prevent my teacher's life from being ruined. After class, I would take a taxi to the psychic's house. I congratulated myself for my excellent plan. *Bravo!*

Still in my striped pajamas, I dialed the psychic's number without delay to make an appointment for that afternoon. The call was answered on the first ring.

"Destiny LaGrande to answer your questions," a female voice said.

"Hello, ma'am. I'd like to make an appointment. Are you available today at four o'clock?"

"I had saved a spot for you. I'll be waiting for you."

Had I heard right? Had she reserved my spot before I even called her? It must have been part of her act, great for making people think she had a genuine gift.

"Then I'll be there," I said.

I hung up. This strange woman intimidated me. My decision to contact her was definitely forcing me out of my comfort zone. Would she think I had lost my mind when she heard my story? For a moment, I felt the urge to call her back and cancel my appointment. But the smiling face of Brianna while she lay on the science teacher's desk came back to haunt me. I resolved to do whatever it took to stop her.

I hurriedly changed into jeans and grabbed a pink blouse. I gave my lioness hair a few strokes with a brush and grabbed my bag. A bowl of cereal was waiting for me on the table, and I devoured my breakfast. Now that I knew what to do, I had my appetite back.

I did my best to avoid Brianna during the day. I really had no desire to run into her. Pretending that nothing had happened was beyond me. I had slept little, and large, dark circles were underlining my eyes. I had tried to cover them up with my mother's concealer. The result was more or less convincing, and I didn't want to have to justify myself to Brianna. Fortunately, there was no danger of my friends worrying about me. They didn't even bother to inquire about me anymore since the party at Lucy's house. They were mostly concerned with Brianna. I had little time for them anyway.

That suited me just fine. I didn't need to explain my dejected look, my tired eyes, and my messy hair.

I spent the day keeping a low profile. I walked close to the hallway walls while glancing left and right to avoid crossing Brianna's path.

I thought I'd gotten away with it when the school bell rang. I was already sighing with relief at the idea of finally being outside the school building. However, I choked up as I closed my locker. Brianna was waiting for me. I'd let my guard down, and she'd got to me. I kicked the metal door discreetly. It was too late to avoid her now.

Brianna approached me. I nodded at her.

"Hello, my friend," she said.

I plastered a smile on my face as she slung her arm over my shoulders. I followed suit. She didn't know I had caught her in the act with a married teacher, and she had her usual rebellious demeanor. There was no guilt on her face. I had really underestimated her. She was even more evil than I had imagined.

"Brianna, I've got to run," I said, pulling away from her. "I've got a dentist appointment. I'll see you later."

"Wait. I wanted to ask you if you wanted to go shopping with me."

I continued walking, pretending not to have heard her. Hoping she would not keep following me, I crossed my fingers and walked with quick and determined steps.

Fortunately, I got rid of her. I sighed with relief. I had felt like a rabbit on the opening day of a hunt. But I had an appointment and no time to lose. I walked a few feet away from the school and Brianna. Finally alone, I pulled my cell phone out of my blue bag and called a cab. I had taken some money out of my emergency fund to pay for transportation and the psychic. The cab arrived quickly.

I opened the taxi door and slid into the back seat. The warmth of the cabin felt nice, as the temperature was dropping on this cloudy autumn afternoon. I rubbed my hands together to warm them.

"So, where am I taking you?" the taxi driver asked.

"I'm going to see the town psychic, Destiny LaGrande. Do you know where it is?"

"Oh yes, of course," he said as we started off. "That old woman has already given my wife the runaround, and she swears by her predictions. I tell her it's all madness and money down the drain. She assures me she sees the future and guides her on her life path. I don't understand any of this nonsense." He shook his head in annoyance.

Leaning back in the seat, I listened distractedly to the driver's speech. I was nervous about meeting the seer. I didn't really want to know more about magic, but unfortunately I couldn't see any other solution.

"After thirty years of marriage, I know when I can change her mind or not. This discussion is hopeless, and I pick my battles, as they say. Don't tell me a teenager like you believes in this stuff? No offense."

His question drew me out of my reverie.

"A short time ago, I would have agreed with you completely, sir," I said. "But with what has happened in my life, I must confess that I don't know what to think anymore."

Disconcerted, he remained silent. I didn't want to rekindle the conversation. His silence allowed me to concentrate on the task at hand. He turned up the volume on the stereo. The trees passed by my window. The houses followed one another, then became more and more scarce as we got closer to Destiny LaGrande's house. I imagined she was a woman who sought isolation. I liked nature but not so much that I would live on the edge of the woods, without even a streetlamp to light the street.

The taxi pulled up in front of a dark alley. I quickly paid the bill and got out. The door slammed behind me, the taxi pulled out, and I found myself alone in the alley. The sun was dropping in the sky, and its rays were becoming less and less able to illuminate the place. The sound of crickets rose in the darkness.

The architecture of the house dated way back. At first glance, I estimated it must have been built a hundred years ago. Despite its age, it was well maintained. Cedar shingles covered the house, typical siding for that era. The door looked like someone had repainted it recently. I had no intention of staying outside any longer. I hurried up the three creaky, wooden steps and knocked on the door. It opened, and I was surprised that it did not make a mournful creak.

An intriguing woman stood before me. Wrinkles covered her face, but she seemed to have a lot of energy. Her hair was long, wavy, and almost completely white. Her eyes were young and sparkling with intelligence. When she looked into my eyes, I felt violated by the intimacy. I felt as if she were reading into the depths of my soul.

I looked down quickly to stop the intrusion. She stepped aside to let me in and closed the door behind me. I found myself in a kitchen well heated by the wood fire burning in the old cast-iron stove.

"Emily, isn't it? I've been waiting for you. Come in, leave

your shoes on the carpet. I don't like to sweep, so I make sure that as little dust as possible gets past my door."

She laughed. I noticed that, unlike the old witches in the stories, she still had all her teeth.

"Give me your coat," she said. "I'll put it right here on this peg, and we can get started."

She took my coat, and I bent down to remove my shoes. She motioned for me to follow her. I entered her well-ordered home. Next to the kitchen was a small room where she received her clients. I could not snoop more in her house because she quickly pulled me into the room and closed the door behind me.

In the room was a round table covered with a white tablecloth. All the walls were white. Candles, also white, illuminated the place with their flickering light. The atmosphere was heavy and muted. A smell that I could not identify came from incense sticks that were slowly burning on a table. Their smoke filled the air and my nostrils.

Destiny crept like a nimble cat behind the round table. She took her place on the imperial seat covered with red, quilted velvet. She motioned for me to take my place on the rough wooden bench opposite her. Although I felt very out of place in this strange setting, I was determined to have the meeting. So I had better sit down.

"So, beautiful, why are you coming to see me tonight?" she asked.

"Well, well, well. It's pretty complicated. I don't know where to start."

"Then let me help you. You want to tell me about a friend of yours."

"No. She's not my friend anymore. She was before I found

out she was doing things… awful things." I swallowed with difficulty.

Emotions overtook me. I was hot, shivering, and had a strange lump in my throat. My hands were sweaty, and I felt like I was about to burst into tears or just pass out. What the hell was happening to me?

"All right, all right," Destiny said. "What'd she do?"

"She uses… powers. She does magic and manipulates everyone around her." I lowered my head in embarrassment. I couldn't believe I had just said that out loud. Destiny might draw cards for a living, but surely she wouldn't believe such an outlandish story.

I didn't dare look up at her. I wrung my hands impatiently, waiting for her to say something.

"Go on."

What? She asked me to continue to tell her my problem? No reaction to what I'd already said?

I put both hands on the table and rose to my feet with a vengeance.

"How can you believe such nonsense? I've seen it with my own eyes and can hardly believe it myself," I said in a whisper.

"There's a lot you don't know yet, honey. I've lived a long time, and I've been in all kinds of situations. Don't think you know everything. You still have some to learn, as well as I do."

I was shocked and relieved at the same time. Feeling I had come to the right place, I got to the heart of the matter. Judging from her initial reaction, she could probably take some more of my story.

"It all seems so unreal," I said. "I don't know how to react. I have to stop her. She's manipulating the entire school to get the best friends and the best grades. Worst of all"—a shiver of disgust ran down my spine as the images invaded my mind—"she seduced our science teacher. He's married! I don't understand her. I'm so disappointed with her attitude."

I stopped to catch my breath. I realized I had thrown out my story and my contempt at full speed, without stopping to breathe.

"I have a solution for you," Destiny said. "However, if you accept, you will have to dedicate a good part of your time to it. It's a long-term commitment, and you'll have to put your heart and soul into it."

I was a little wary of her "solution." I felt that the moment I agreed to her proposal, my world would be turned upside down. Hadn't it already shifted when I'd seen Brianna and Mr. Thompson together in the classroom?

I had come to this woman hoping that she could help me solve my problem. Now that she was offering to help, I was hesitant.

Destiny looked at me with an indecipherable expression. Despite my uncertainty, I had no choice. Brianna was using her knowledge to manipulate others, and I couldn't let her.

"I've made up my mind," I said. "I must do what I can to stop her."

"All right then. I can teach you a few things about disabling her spells. You'll have to tell me exactly what she's using to cast them, and we'll study possible methods to counteract them. Your learning will have to become your top priority."

I nodded my head to show that I understood.

"I warn you that although I have expert knowledge of magic and a well-stocked library, I have only limited powers. I hope you have better magical potential than I do, because if not, there's nothing we can do to stop it."

I was puzzled. I had supposed that any of us could perform spells, that the *recipe* worked for anyone, as long as they followed the steps to the letter. It seemed not. I realized how little I knew about this parallel world I had just discovered and stepped into against my better judgment.

"How can I evaluate my magical potential?" I asked.

"We'll find out as you master the spells I teach you. Let's hope you're more disciplined and powerful than your friend. Only then will you be able to stop her. What's her name anyway?"

"Brianna Ducharme."

"A Ducharme descendant!" Destiny said. "Interesting. I thought the bloodline died out decades ago."

She reached for her bookcase and was already browsing through an ancient book.

"Who are the Ducharmes?" I asked, hoping to corroborate the information I had gleaned from the Internet.

"It's a lineage that goes back hundreds of years. Originated in Ireland. Many of them emigrated to the United States. You know the history of Salem?"

"Of course."

"Ducharmes have perished by the fire. But only some women develop magical potential, although men carry the gene and can pass it on. A few of the men are sorcerers, and they are extremely powerful."

"But then how can women pass on the name Ducharme if only women are witches?" I had read the answer, but I was testing Destiny.

"Daughters who are born to a woman with this name and who display magic abilities receive their mother's name. Other children, regardless of their gender, are named after their father."

"I imagine that was unusual in a patriarchal society of the Middle Ages," I said. "And even today."

"Since the beginning of time, witches have been persecuted. People fear them. But they live by their own code. Their secret society displays more feminine values."

These revelations gave me pause, but Destiny seemed eager to get back to Brianna's case. "Is she well trained?"

"How should I know?"

"Give me all the information you have on this girl. Every detail counts." She got up and fetched a leather-bound notebook. She opened it and took a pen to write down everything I said.

"Brianna is my age, with red hair and piercing green eyes," I said. "I know she's been living with her aunt recently. She once told me she was living with her to learn more about magic, but at the time, I took that statement with a grain of salt. She is so different! Also, I went to her house. Her aunt has an array of weirder objects in her house."

"Oh yeah? What did you see?"

"I don't remember everything… jars, metal boxes, old leather-bound books, dried herbs I couldn't identify. Stuff like that."

"Classic," Destiny said, without looking up from her notebook. She furiously scribbled down every detail I gave her.

"I saw Brianna do some spells. One to make a boy fall in love with me."

"How could you do that? You can't do such a thing! People must have free will!"

"But I never thought it would work. Anyway," I said, ashamed, "I asked Brianna to remove the spell. And let's just say it worked."

"Tell me how she did it so I can analyze her style."

I searched my memory for as many details as I could and told them to her.

"Okay, what else?" Destiny asked.

"I wasn't there when she did her other spells, but I noticed some strange changes at the school. First, the students suddenly started liking her."

"A popularity charm. Quite typical of a teenage girl who practices black magic."

"What! But she always told me she was only interested in white magic."

Or had I taken that for granted? I couldn't remember.

"Don't be naïve, my dear," she said, clicking her tongue. "White magic is for good and not for evil. Brianna is shamelessly using magic for her own benefit. It can only be dark magic. What else could it be?"

I was astonished. I thought about her words. Indeed, what she was saying made sense.

"She received an invitation to the hottest party in school, and that was without being friends with Lucy, the girl who organized the party." I summoned the courage to continue. "Finally, the most disgusting thing she did is she seduced our fascinating science teacher, Mr. Thompson, who's married! She has no conscience."

"I can see that this action has shocked you."

"Yes. I saw them together."

"But you took advantage of her other spells, didn't you?" Destiny asked.

"Yes. I felt it was wrong, but it was so intoxicating. I finally had all the attention and friendship I could want." Ashamed, I lowered my head. I knew I had done wrong.

Destiny closed her notebook in a great theatrical movement. She leaned toward me, her expression very serious. The candles cast ominous shadows on her face.

"If you become my student, you must swear to use magic only for good. You cannot use your knowledge to give yourself an unfair advantage over others. You will face difficult situations, but what I am about to show you must not be used as a dark tool. Do you understand me?"

"Yes."

"So, swear on your most precious thing!" Destiny said.

"I swear on my sister's head!"

"Perfect," she said, jumping to her feet.

She walked out of the stuffy room and into her kitchen. I followed, wondering what she was up to. She walked to a door and opened it to reveal a large room filled with dusty, old books. A musty smell filled my nostrils.

"This is a book for beginners," Destiny said. "I have mastered all the spells inside."

She threw the book into my arms. I opened the book at random and flipped through a few pages.

"I'll lend it to you until next week. Study and learn them," she said. "Also, get a notebook and record everything you find out about Brianna. I want to know what kind of witch we're dealing with. Some witches can be powerful, and I hope that's not the case with this Brianna. Otherwise, only heaven can help us."

She pushed me out of her library. Apparently, our talk was over. I took my things and the book. I went out to get into the taxi she had already called for me.

On the way home, I thought back to my meeting with the psychic. We had an appointment the following Saturday. That gave me little time to look through the hundred-page book that sat on my lap, study for my math exam, and spy on Brianna.

I had wished for a more exciting life, and now I was being granted more excitement than I wanted.

Once I was safely in my room, I settled under the covers with a pad of paper and a pen. Although I was sleepy after such an eventful day, I had to make a precise list of everything I would need for my new double life as a witch's apprentice. I got lucky because my mother had invited me to go shopping the next day. I had to be prepared.

I consulted Destiny's book to find out what equipment I would need to practice the spells she had asked me to experiment with. There were many tools and ingredients I would need. I started a list. The longer my list grew, the more I had to face the fact that I would have to dip into my savings once again to buy everything on it. I sighed in resignation.

On Thursday night, I was ready for my shopping trip. I had found a good reason to separate myself from my mother once we got to the shopping mall. I wouldn't have known what to say to her to justify buying multiple candles, herbs, pots, daggers, and other weird stuff.

Fortunately, I found everything quickly. I was relieved. I hadn't thought it would be so easy. Maybe this time my luck was going to change for good.

My cell phone vibrated in my blue purse, so I pulled it out. It was a text from William.

I'm looking forward to our meeting. I'll pick you up at seven.

Oh, damn it! With all this going on, I had completely forgotten about my date with William. I had nothing to wear. Panicked, I went into a store to find a top for the outing.

It was getting late, and I had to meet my mother. I hid my strange purchases as best as I could, under some hastily purchased clothing. So when my mother, curious, asked to see my purchases, she saw only the sweaters and not the objects hidden underneath. I congratulated myself on my deception.

I pushed her toward the exit. "Mom, I completely forgot to tell you. I have a date tonight."

"Oh, yeah? How could you forget! With whom?"

"With William."

"William? You never told me about him."

"He was with us in Montreal for the crystal contest."

"Emily! I wish you would have told me about this before. And on a Thursday, a weeknight. You know very well that I don't agree with you staying up late on school nights."

"Come on, Mom. I want to go! I already said yes."

"Where are you going?" she asked.

"To the movies. Nothing dangerous or criminal."

She sighed. I could feel that she was about to give in. "All right. But I want to meet him before you go out. And you have to be back by ten o'clock at the latest. Then straight to bed."

"Okay, we'll go to the seven-thirty showing. No problem."

I was willing to accept all her conditions, as long as she let me go out.

"William will be here at seven," I said.

With that out of the way, I chatted absentmindedly with my mother on the way home. I couldn't help but look forward to trying out all the spells I had discovered yesterday. During my reading, I had selected some and designed a tight schedule so I wouldn't overlook anything. I planned five of them to get the hang of it today. One to chase away bad luck. One to ensure protection and to be done for each member of my family. One to attract prosperity—selfish, but since it was part of the book given to me by Destiny, I guess she approved of it despite her warning. One to find out if I was a victim of a spell. And the last one to elicit premonitory dreams, which could prove to be very useful.

I rushed to my room and locked the door. My mother must have been used to my secrecy, for she asked me no questions. I set to work without delay.

I began with the spell to chase away bad luck, for it was the simplest—though rather strange. I lit some white candles and placed them in a circle on the floor. Carefully, I secured the whole thing, for I had no desire to set the house on fire. How ironic it would be to set the house on fire because of a bad luck spell.

I lit the rose incense as instructed in the book and pushed it toward the four cardinal points. Then I took a glass jar and layered the following objects in it—rusty nails from the garage, pins, broken dishes, and stones. I closed the jar and sealed it with wax. I recited a few words while blowing incense on the pot.

I was satisfied when I looked at the container in the candle-light. My new profession was working for me. I had done all the steps thoroughly, but how could I tell if I had done it right? I wasn't a clumsy girl by nature, so I might never really know if my spell worked, let alone be able to evaluate my power.

I moved on to the second spell on the program, the one to attract protection. I needed a new pot, but the candles had already been laid out on the floor. *How effective!* Performing the spells one after the other was saving time.

I wrote the names of each member of my family by hand on yellow pieces of paper. After placing each piece at the jar's bottom, I said the magic incantation written in the grimoire.

"Protect this person who means a lot to me."

My mother called me for supper, I hadn't noticed the time

pass. I shouted from my room that I was not hungry. I would not interrupt my study session on magic since I only had half an hour before William arrived.

I went back to the spell, adding a pinch each of salt, basil, sage, sesame seeds, garlic powder, and pepper. The smell of the mixture was disconcerting. I thought for a moment that smoke was rising from the pot because the scent was so strong. I shook my head vigorously to bring myself back to reality. It was impossible. I might believe in magic now, but my rational mind was still wide awake and struggling to explain what was happening.

The last instructions of the spell told me to hide the jar in a place where it would never be moved. I would hide it in the back of the basement closet. It was an indescribable mess, and no one would find it there.

"Emily!" My mother called. "William is here."

Oh no! I really hadn't noticed the time go by.

I hastily extinguished the candles and put them away on the shelf of my white bookcase, making sure they touched nothing so the house wouldn't go up in smoke. I walked out of my room and opened the closet door. I sighed with discouragement at the mess. I placed the jar as deep into the closet as possible, reaching between objects and pushing it into the mess.

I rubbed my hands together with satisfaction to shake off the dust. Two spells cast without a hitch. I'd had a productive evening.

Back in my room, I rummaged through the bags from the store to find the sweater I had bought specifically for my date with William. I ripped off the tag, hurriedly put it on, hastily applied mascara, and grabbed my bag as I left my room. I brushed my hair with my fingers as I raced up the stairs.

William was in the hallway being interrogated by my parents. My sister was running around the living room with her favorite doll, pretending it was flying like a superhero.

"Hi, William," I said. "Let's go. We're gonna be late for the movie."

I grabbed William's arm with a little too much vigor and dashed for the exit, hoping to avoid a prolonged conversation with my parents. They could only embarrass me.

"Just a moment, Emily. I'd like to know a little more about William," my mother said.

William turned to her.

"Emily told me you also took part in the crystal contest?"

"Yes, Ms. Reed. But we didn't do as well as Emily and Brianna," William said. "I love science."

My mother chuckled approvingly. I knew she would embarrass me. My cheeks burned.

My father joined in. "Are you serious about school? Do you turn in your homework on time? Do you get good grades?"

Misery! My father asked all his questions in an unsympathetic tone, like an undercover special force agent. I took William's side.

"Daddy! There's nothing wrong with William," I said. "I understand he's doing very well in school. Anyway, we're only going to the movies, so you don't need to know his GPA."

Decisively, I led William toward the door once more. My parents must have been pleased because they didn't stop us a second time.

"Good evening, Mr. and Mrs. Reed," William said quickly before I closed the door.

Once outside, William wiped a bead of sweat from his forehead. William's mother's car, a black Nissan that was already a few years old, was parked in front of the house. I strode purposefully to the car, still reeling from the awkward exchange.

My thoughts distracted me the whole way. I couldn't stop pondering about Brianna. William was attempting to keep the conversation going, which I punctuated with "um" and "yeah."

I was in a dull mood and didn't really want to see a romantic movie. Fortunately, William let me select an action movie, *Iron Man*. I immediately headed for the popcorn.

"Are you hungry?" William asked.

"Of course," I said. After all, I hadn't had dinner.

William ordered us each popcorn, a chocolate bar and a soft drink. *My favorite foods!*

For over an hour, the explosions blinded me, dazed me, and left me half deaf. I was completely immersed in the story when William took my hand in his. It was warm. I looked at him, my face feeling as red as a peony, as I left my hand in his. He gave me a radiant smile with his beautiful white teeth. My heart pounded. How lucky was I? This handsome guy was interested in me.

When the movie was over, William did not let go of my hand. He led me to the car, and I heard the locks being released.

On the way home, I was too embarrassed to speak. Normally I would have liked to discuss the movie, but William had made me forget about it so quickly. He was driving with one hand, the other still holding mine.

When we arrived at my house, he parked the car and leaned over to me. A warm feeling came over me. I closed my eyes and leaned toward him. I saw stars. He was a much better kisser than Christian.

"Thank you for a lovely evening, Emily," he said simply,

flashing a beautiful smile.

"Thank you for inviting me," I said happily.

I got out and closed the door. William started the car and drove away. I floated out the door.

"Emily!" my mother said when I entered the house. "You're right on time."

My parents were waiting for me—of course—comfortably seated on the sofa. They were eating popcorn and watching a movie.

I sat down beside them and told them vaguely about my evening with William, barely holding back the smug smile that constantly threatened to cross my lips.

"He seems nice. I like him better than Christian," my father said.

"Stephen!" my mother said, nudging him with her elbow.

"Go to bed now," my father said.

I went down to my room and made myself comfortable on my bed. Dreamily, I thought of the wonderful evening I had spent with William. I was on cloud nine. I had butterflies in my stomach. He had been very kind, and I loved the taste of his lips. I touched my own lips, remembering his kiss. A quick glance at my alarm clock brought me back to reality. It was 10:23 p.m. *Damn it!* I'd almost forgotten about my problems with Brianna. Even though it was getting late, I had to continue my magical studies, and the next three spells seemed a bit more complicated to my beginner's eyes.

Determined, I opened the book to the right page.

"Let us now attract prosperity," I said with a sigh.

Destiny had made it clear that I was not to use my powers for personal gain. So why did this spell exist? Since I didn't want Destiny to reprimand me, I needed to cast the spell for someone else's benefit. Who to choose? If I chose a family member, I would take advantage of the prosperity, too, so that wasn't right either. Why not choose my neighbor Sylvie Reed then? She was nice. She had taken care of me a few times when I was little and my mother had an emergency to deal with. She always greeted me when I passed her in the neighborhood. Since her husband had left her alone with two children, I guessed she had little money to pay her bills and spoil her little girls. I made my choice.

Satisfied, I analyzed the required materials. *Damn it!* I needed a picture of my neighbor,

I went on the Internet to find her. On Facebook, I had access to her profile picture after a few clicks of the mouse. I selected the photo to copy and enlarged it. Perfect to do my spell. I printed the photo out in color and trimmed the edges.

I had to use green candles instead of white ones because apparently green is the color that represented prosperity. I lit four candles and arranged them at the four cardinal points—north, south, east, and west.

I took a green pen and traced a $ sign across the four corners of my neighbor's picture. In a small, green-velvet bag, I placed four corn seeds, four sesame seeds, four oatmeal seeds, and finally, four peppercorns. I folded the photo in half, then in half again—forming four parts—and placed it in the bag under my pillow. By the end of the seventh day, my neighbor was supposed to receive her gift. I couldn't wait to see what would happen to her, and I smiled as I thought of my good deed. Now I just had to see the result.

I blew out the green candles and lit purple ones. My book said that the color purple increased psychic ability. I guessed the purple candles would help me find out if Brianna had put me under an enchantment spell. I performed the same ritual as I had before, placing the candles at the four cardinal points to form my magic circle.

Then I poured water into a deep glass bowl and recited an incantation aloud.

"Clear water, reveal to me if someone is playing with me. Show me if I am a victim of a spell."

I got a picture of myself and slipped it into the water. To my surprise, my image faded away. I was shocked. The good news was that I had undoubtedly succeeded in the spell. The bad news was that I was the victim of a spell. I was boiling with rage at the thought of Brianna doing such a thing to me. I would not sit back and do nothing.

I sprang to my feet and paced the room like a caged tigress. I could hardly contain myself. Why did she put a spell on me? What did she want me to do? Was this the cause of our friendship? I couldn't figure out why she wanted to put a spell on me unless it was to manipulate me.

As I was not calming down at all, I took out my diary and angrily wrote everything that was going through my mind. My rage at discovering that I was a victim of a spell. My disappointment at Brianna's behavior—how I had wished to be her friend and how much she had fooled me. My desire to get back to a normal life and to forget all about magic, both white and black.

It took me an hour to calm down. My pencil was running out of steam, and I felt that I had regained control of myself. I still had work to do, and this was not the time to give up.

Finally, I was ready for the last spell selected for the day— the one to induce premonitory dreams.

All I had to do was put a few drops of essential oil on a piece of absorbent cloth and place it a few inches from my nose while I slept. I opened a small bottle of jasmine essential oil. I put two drops on the cloth, which absorbed it greedily. It smelled great. I opened the second bottle, which contained lavender essential oil. Again, I dropped two drops on the cloth. The smell was a little more pleasant but very strong. The last bottle was St. John's wort. The combination was intense and unpleasant. I had no choice but to get used to it, since the book told me that the smell could last for months and that I would have to sleep while breathing the mixture.

It was past midnight when I ended my magic session. I made sure the candles were out and hid all the items in my closet. My eyelids were heavy, but I felt a great sense of satisfaction. The smell of essential oils filled my nostrils, but luckily I was so exhausted that I fell asleep quickly.

The next day, I woke up disappointed. I had had no premonitory dreams. Did that mean the spell hadn't worked? That I didn't have magical powers? Or just that I didn't remember the dreams? I chuckled with annoyance. How convenient would it be to have premonitory dreams if you couldn't remember them when you woke up? I kicked my pillow. It was frustrating to have so many questions and no answers. I had to be patient.

The following Sunday, I had breakfast with my mother. My father had already left to go shopping with my sister. I ate my cereal in silence. My mother didn't mind. She wasn't a morning person either and did not talk much before her second cup of coffee. Normally that bothered me, but today it suited me. I wasn't thinking clearly enough to face an interrogation.

I had planned nothing that day. It was a rather chilly day for the season. I decided it would be better for me to spend some time studying for my upcoming English exam and also to continue reading the book Destiny had lent me.

The week went on like that. My life was taking an unreal turn. Between studying magic, practicing spells, going to classes, doing homework, and taking exams, there was no time left for anything else.

I had confronted Brianna after I found out she had cast a spell on me. She had denied everything. We hadn't spoken since, and as a result, I was often left alone.

Brianna was pursuing her life as she saw fit. She knew I didn't approve of her choices. Seeing her strut down the school hallways made me sick. When I passed her, she either ignored me completely or gave me a knowing wink, as if I were complicit in her behavior. This attitude made me furious.

Would I have to endure this for the rest of high school?

The days passed. On Thursday, Halloween, a lot of excitement was in the air at school. The student council members were having a card sale. We had the whole day to write to our friends, and then the council members would distribute the cards at the end of the afternoon, during the last class.

Students rushed to the table set up for the event, choosing cards adorned with witches, monsters, zombies, and spiders. Adding to the excitement, tomorrow night there would be a big Halloween party for all the students in the cafeteria. Everybody was laughing and discussing what costumes they'd wear for the occasion.

I was not in the mood to celebrate. Although I would receive tons of cards because of my newfound popularity, I knew that none of them would be genuine. It was all because of Brianna's magic.

When the time came, I took with feigned joy the stack of

cards handed to me by the vice president of the student council. I was unfolding each card with little interest when one caught my eye. It was from William.

Dear Emily,
I'm not good with words, so I'll just ask you.
Will you go to the Halloween party with me?
William

Blushing, I happily closed the card and put it back in the box. Even though I had spent little time with him, William was still thinking about me. Suddenly panicked, I realized I didn't even have a costume for the party, since I'd had no intention of going. The bell rang.

Brianna joined me at my locker.

"Come on, old friend," she said. "Let's forget the past. You'll have to get used to the idea anyway. You can't do anything to stop me. Why not enjoy this life I've created for us?"

I didn't answer since I was done arguing with my only real friend. I had spent the entire week alone, avoiding her in the cafeteria, the computer room, the library, and even the bathroom. A hellish week.

She must have felt my resistance melt away because she invited me to her house. "I've got some great costumes at home for the party tomorrow. Don't worry about a thing!"

I smiled. Because of her, my life was no longer lacking in spice. Had it really been Brianna in the room with Mr. Thompson? The images were blurry in my head, and I had run away so quickly that I suddenly wasn't sure I had seen right. Maybe I'd done my incantation wrong and wasn't actually under the influence of one of her spells. I was tired of wandering around the school corridors, invisible to everyone, like a ghost.

As planned, I prepared for the party in her room. I had accepted William's invitation. We were to meet directly at the school.

Brianna was yapping like a magpie. She was obviously thrilled to be out and about.

"I have a companion too. But it's a secret. You'll find out who it is tonight," she said with a wink.

I hoped she would not be so bold as to show off with Mr. Thompson, the married science teacher. Deciding that I was going to enjoy my evening, I shook my head at that gloomy thought.

Brianna reached into the back of her closet and pulled out two identical… witchy disguises. She never ceased to surprise me.

Black knee-high boots with dizzying heels, a black minidress with thin straps, and a pointed hat with a wide brim. *Wow!* We were going to be the center of attention at the party.

I rushed to the costume and put it on. Brianna did the same. Then she put on my makeup, which was outrageous. A thick black line highlighted my eyes, and mascara plastered my eyelashes. While she was applying her own makeup, I put on the long, leather boots. I placed the hat on my long, brown hair.

"All that's missing is the last accessory," Brianna said.

She turned to a large chest at the back of the room. She took out two rods carved into wood.

"Are these real magic wands?" I asked in disbelief.

"Don't be ridiculous," she said.

So they were fake. A little disappointed, I took the one she handed me. I wished I had a magic wand in my hands.

"Of course they are authentic!" Brianna said.

I choked with surprise.

"They have been passed down from generation to generation, so watch out for them," she said. "Wands are not as trendy anymore, I must admit. I don't really know how to use them. I prefer rituals and incantations."

I inspected my wand more closely. Nothing caught my eye. I made a mental note to ask Destiny about it the next time we met.

Brianna came to join me, and we stood in front of the large mirror in her room.

"Wow!" I said.

Brianna was obviously gloating. With good reason. We were going to be the stars of this evening, manipulation or not.

She grabbed her cell phone to take a picture of us before we left.

"Let's go, my friend!" Brianna said. "Let the party begin!"

Brianna's aunt dropped us off at the party, which was already in full swing.

The entire school was dark, except for the cafeteria. Through the window, we could see orange lights swinging back and forth, strobe lights coming on and off, all in a festive mood. The music was playing loud enough for us to hear from outside. A chilly breeze passed over us, assaulted my bare knees, and slid wildly under my coat, pushing me toward the door.

At the entrance, two students from the student council greeted us, one dressed as Superman and the other as a cat. Shivering, I paid the entrance fee, and the cat stamped a pumpkin image on the back of my hand.

In the cafeteria, decorated with orange and black garlands,

there were groups of students in every corner. Many were yelling over the music, while a few more daring ones were on the dance floor. Brianna and I weaved in and out of the crowd, drawing all eyes. I smiled. It was so good to be popular. I walked with pride, clicking my high heels on the floor, as if I were an international model walking down a catwalk. Like in the chick flicks, it felt like everything was happening in slow motion, including my hair moving around my face as I walked. It was so cool. I could really get a taste for this kind of life. I smiled at Brianna.

I was looking around for William when someone behind me clamped two hands over my eyes.

"Guess who it is," a teenager said in a scary, rumbling voice.

"William, let me go!" I said, laughing.

"How did you recognize me so easily? I changed my voice," he said, sounding disappointed.

He looked very sexy in his woodsman costume of a cape, boots, a red plaid shirt, orange suspenders, and a fake beard.

I placed a quick kiss on his rough cheek.

He smiled at me, delighted. "You are beautiful, little witch."

"You too," I said, blushing, surprised at the compliment.

"I'll leave you lovers. Someone is waiting for me," Brianna said loudly over the noise of the music.

I blushed. William and I hadn't yet reached the point of calling each other "lovers." I watched Brianna slip away into the crowd.

"Would you like something to drink?" William asked. "Juice, pop, or water? That's what's on the menu tonight."

With a gentle hand on my back, he guided me to the small window where students were waiting to order. In line, I couldn't concentrate on what William was telling me. Curiosity consumed me as I searched the crowd for Brianna. The strobe lights blinded me, and I couldn't see. She had to be somewhere.

"Are you listening to me, Emily?" William asked.

"Uh-huh. What? Yes, yes. Of course!"

He was not at all convinced. I could see it on his face.

"I was just telling you about my badminton tournament," William said. "It's a very important tournament."

"What can I do for you?" A student disguised as a peasant woman in a white bonnet, a big beige dress, and a white apron was smiling at us. We had reached the front of the line.

"A Pepsi diet for me," I said.

"A Pepsi for me," William said.

William settled the bill for both of us.

"Thank you," I said, uncapping the can.

"To your health," he said, clinking his can with mine.

We slipped through the growing crowd to join his group of friends. I was still looking for Brianna, who was nowhere to be found.

"I'm going to the bathroom. Will you wait for me here?" I said into William's ear.

"I won't move," he said, placing a soft kiss on my cheek.

I felt my heart racing. I thought I could really fall in love with him

Happily, I made my way to the bathroom. The crowd was thickening, and I struggled to make my way through the sea of people.

That was when I saw her. Brianna was leaning against a boy, sandwiching him against the wall. They were kissing passionately, his hands kneading her buttocks ardently. She was rubbing herself on him languidly. *In public!* Brianna was decidedly unashamed.

I approached to find out the identity of her mysterious date. My heart leapt in my chest when I recognized him.

Christian.

She was dating Christian Davis.

How could she do this to me?

At that very moment, she turned away from him. Her green eyes focused on mine.

In a panic, I rushed to the bathroom. I frantically rummaged through my bag to get my phone.

"Hello?" came a voice at the other end of the line.

"Mommy? Mommy! Come and get me now," I said, whimpering.

"Emily? What's the matter? Are you hurt? Are you all right?"

I adopted a more normal voice to reassure her. "Don't worry. I'm fine. Just come get me. I'll be waiting for you at the cafeteria door. Remember which one?"

"Yes, yes. No problem. I'll be right there." She hung up.

I came out of the bathroom and ran toward William. My eyes were acclimatizing again to the darkness in the room.

"William, I have to go," I said. "Thanks for the evening. See you Monday."

"Come on, Emily. What's the matter? Why are you leaving so early?"

I gave him the first excuse that came to mind. "I forgot that I actually have to work on a project for chemistry class. Bye, guys."

I placed a quick kiss on his cheek. A hand closed on my arm as I left.

"Emily, are you leaving already?" Brianna said, sneering.

That was all I needed. I tried to pull my arm free, but she held on.

"Since it didn't work out with you and Christian, I didn't think you'd mind if I went out with him." She was explaining all this to me with an air of complete innocence, twisting a lock of her red hair.

What a bitch!

"That's what you really thought! You could have at least warned me. You know I still like Christian Davis."

It was then that I realized William was right next to me and had heard every word. I turned to him, sorry. "William, wait. That's not what I meant."

Already he was turning away.

"William!"

He did not turn around. Why would he? I had really screwed up.

Brianna was beaming with joy. My misfortune was obviously making her happy. Had she been planning this all along?

"You think you're so smart, you witch!" I told Brianna. "I know very well that in normal circumstances, Christian would never be interested in you. You can keep your artificial love."

I couldn't bear to look at her face one more second. Enraged, I bolted for the locker room, where I retrieved my coat. As I pushed open the glass door, salty tears rolled down my cheeks. My mother's car was just pulling into the parking lot. I rushed over to the car and opened the door before my mother had time to come to a complete stop.

"Emily, what's going on?" she asked.

"Drive, Mom. Drive, please! I just want to get out of here as soon as possible."

She pressed the accelerator. I buried my face in my scarf, which was soaked with my silent tears weighed down with mascara.

"Sweetheart, talk to me. What happened?"

I opened the glove compartment to get some tissues. I wiped my nose clean and dried my tears. I finally answered her question.

"Brianna," I said, sniffing. "She was all over Christian."

"Um… She seems to get all the boys she wants. And Christian, do you still like him?"

"Maybe… I don't know! I have William now. It's just…"

I paused. I didn't know how to explain what I was feeling.

"William seems like a nice boy, Emily," my mother said. "But do you really like him?"

She had just asked an excellent question. Despite all his good qualities, William didn't make my heart beat as fast as I would have hoped. I wasn't ready to face reality.

My mother did not insist on an answer. "Think about it. You don't have to decide right now. You'll see more clearly tomorrow."

She parked in front of the house.

"Thanks for picking me up," I said. "Thanks for always being there for me."

Exhausted, I went to my room, took off my witch costume, and threw it on the floor. Without even removing my makeup, I slipped under the covers of my bed.

What an evening!

Chapter 8

November started with below-normal temperatures. It was freezing cold. As expected, I found myself at Destiny's door with her book under my arm. I was proud of my self-discipline, but I was doubting my magical abilities and had a list of questions running through my head. I knocked on the door, hopping from one foot to the other to warm up. I hoped Destiny would open the door quickly so I could finally get out of the cold.

"Come in, my little one," Destiny said when she swung open the door. "Come and warm yourself by the fire."

I shivered my way through the doorframe and took off my blue mittens. I desperately rubbed my hands together to warm them. Destiny relieved me of my coat and handed me a cup of steaming hot chocolate. I took it gratefully.

She motioned for me to sit by her wood stove. She had arranged two old rocking chairs before the flames. They were from another era, with faded wooden cradles and sinewy seats covered with flattened, faded cushions. As I sat on one of the chairs, I noticed it creaked with every rocking motion, which didn't surprise me at all. I was stunned, however, to find the worn chair so comfortable.

I handed the book of magic to Destiny.

"Have you been practicing?" she asked. "Did you read everything? Any results?"

Her eyes were shining with excitement. I hadn't thought she would be so eager to hear about my progress. I realized with relief that I was no longer alone in this adventure.

"I've cast several spells this week." I related my experiments, and the results I'd gotten—or rather, the absence of results.

"Don't let this discourage you." Destiny rummaged through the pile of books and papers on the coffee table. "I can't determine the strength of your powers after only a week of training. The results are relative, especially for the type of spells you cast. It's a complex journey, and it's too early to interpret anything."

I didn't dare ask, but why had she wasted my time with these spells then? As if she could read my mind—or was my face an open book?—she continued talking.

"You had to start with these spells to familiarize yourself with the process. Learn to walk before you run!" Destiny said. "Every move you make counts. You must understand that it is better to make mistakes with inconsequential experiments. However, as I see that you have studied well, I can lend you an extremely rare, ancient book I keep in my private library. My great-grandmother's mother got it from a mage who was crazy in the village. Since then, we have passed it down from generation to generation."

She straightened in her chair, leaning on her arms to aid her in standing. Her demeanor made her look weak and tired. She walked over to the shelves, which were overflowing with books, and she reached out, rose on tiptoe, and grabbed a volume. It looked antique indeed. She came back to me. Hesitantly, she handed the book to me.

"Take great care of it."

Intrigued, I handled the thick book with respect. Its pages were yellowed and brittle, and its brown leather binding showed many signs of wear.

"Turn to page ten," she said.

I placed the book on the weathered wooden table and turned the pages gently. I glimpsed at the hand-drawn pictures. Notes carefully handwritten in cursive pencil accumulated in the margins. These discoveries fascinated and intrigued me, but for the moment, I stuck to the instructions given to me by Destiny. I reached page ten.

"I ask you to go through the pages of this book over the next week," Destiny said. "You may try some rituals but only those in the first two chapters, the ones that help to purify the witch. You must do none of the other spells, as they can be dangerous if you don't master them properly."

She lifted my chin to force me to look into her eyes. I immediately felt uncomfortable with this forced contact, but I did not look away.

"Swear to me you will not try any spell after chapter two," she said.

"I promise!" I said immediately so that she would let me go.

She looked friendly again, as if nothing had happened.

"Starting on page ten, you will find a lot of tips on how to improve your technique," she said. "Once you have completed the study of this book, you will come back here, and we will do some tests. They will show us the true potential of your magic."

Destiny slipped the book into a hemp bag and tidied up the table. I realized that our talk was over. As I got up to leave, I remembered a question. It was now burning in my mind.

"Destiny, what do you know about magic wands?" I asked.

She stopped and stared at me in disbelief. "Magic wands? Ha! But nobody uses them anymore."

"Brianna has them at home. In fact, I can say that she has at least two, maybe more. One of them is in my possession, on the floor of my room."

"How is that possible?"

Ashamed of my carelessness, I looked down. "Yes, I know. I should've taken better care of—"

"Emily, I don't care where you put the wand," she said, cutting me off sharply. "I want to know what Brianna told you about them."

"Um," I said, trying to remember. "Let's see. What words did she use exactly?"

Destiny was getting impatient. "Tell me!"

"That the wands had been passed down from generation to generation but that no one used them anymore. That the tradition had been lost."

Destiny rushed to her bookcase, which was overflowing with books. She pulled up a stool. She climbed onto it, balancing precariously, and reached for a huge, dusty book that was on the highest shelf. Her balance looked off, and I thought for a moment that she would fall, but fortunately, she regained her footing.

She blew on the book, and a gray cloud of dust flew up. She coughed. "God, I really should clean up more often. These shelves are so hard to reach. I should get one of those dusting things with the telescopic handle. But I digress."

She looked at the book with interest.

"I'd almost forgotten about this book. *Magic Wands and Consecrations*," she said, squinting to decipher the title. "There's a lot of information in here about wands, but you're wasting your time. If wands aren't used anymore, then they're not as needed as they seem."

She put the precious book in the bag. I put on my coat and boots. I took the package and clutched it to my chest, as if to protect it from the cold. The taxi was waiting for me to go home.

I was anxious and excited to measure my magical powers and learn more about this world that was still unknown to me. I felt it was my duty to stop Brianna, but I wasn't interested in the power. I was even a little afraid of it. What if it turned me into someone I didn't like, willing to do anything for my own happiness and to manipulate others the same way Brianna was doing? I didn't want to become like her. I winced at the thought.

In the warmth of my room, shaken by my encounter with Destiny and exhausted by an arduous week in class, I couldn't find the courage to read, despite my great curiosity. I crawled under my thick blankets and fell asleep immediately.

The timid rays of the autumn sun slipped through the curtains and roused me from my heavy sleep. Although I had slept for nearly ten hours, I found it difficult to get out of bed. My cat slipped through the half-open door of my room, jumped on my bed and rubbed his head on my face insistently. He purred furiously to get my attention—and to get petted. I finally let his cute face charm me. With my eyes barely open, I petted him. He rolled onto his back happily, purring more and more. I scratched his belly, laughing.

Ken jumped onto my bedside table. I followed him with my eyes to find that he was standing on Destiny's book.

"Ken, go away," I said to chase him away.

Insulted, Ken left my room. Distracted, I reached for the

book, which must have been over a hundred years old. I flipped through it. There was so much information in the new book that Destiny had given me. The first few chapters covered mostly the history of magic in the world. The oldest writings found dated back to ancient Rome, but the legends were from much further back. I straightened up on my bed, placed my pillow behind my back, and immersed myself in the reading.

It was fascinating. The stories featured a few spells, and I tried a few. The rest was much more difficult to comprehend, and information was coming out of my ears. Sentences were heavier, denser, and I had to reread certain passages several times to make sense of them.

I closed the book. A cloud of dust flew out, and I coughed. I put it back on my bedside table. My head was overflowing with information.

The costume Brianna had lent me for Halloween caught my eye. It was lying jumbled on the floor of my room. The wand was tangled up in it. I bent down to pick up the wand and inspect it. There was nothing to distinguish it from a common branch. It was about twenty inches long and had been made from a thin tree branch and carefully sanded.

I put it on my bedside table and grabbed the book on wands that Destiny had lent me. This book was even older than the others. The title *Magic Wands and Consecrations*, embossed on the black leather cover, was faded with age. I handled it with great care. Its yellowed and cracking pages smelled musty, and the writing was disappearing in places. I read.

The wand is a very important tool in the art of white magic. Besides mixing the contents of the cauldron and drawing the circle of protection, it is used to concentrate and direct our energies to a very specific point. This incredible weapon represents the element of fire and symbolizes the strength, conviction, and power of the witch or wizard who wields it. It is the link between the human being and the cosmic forces. Therefore, it is an indispensable tool in the practice of magic.

"The author apparently did not know that the use of wands would fall out of custom," I said aloud. I continued reading.

Each wizard must make his own wand from a branch found during a solitary walk in the forest. The type of wood chosen will help him better channel his powers. For example, maple is particularly recommended for prosperity and love rituals. Skilled magicians have several types of wands, which are specific to certain uses.

To aid in the identification and classification of wands, a section of the index lists the ten most commonly used species, although all trees have interesting characteristics for the practice of magic.

I turned the pages to discover the indicated passage. There was a lot of information—the scientific names of the species, drawings of the leaves and bark, the territories where they grew, and more. Finally, I found a black-and-white photo of what the manufactured sticks of each tree species looked like. I opened a lamp and brought Brianna's wand close to the book. It was really hard to tell. I was hesitating between two species in particular—oak and elm.

I looked up the characteristics of wands using those types of wood. In short, oak was used in druidic rituals and solar magic, while elm was used for protection rituals. I wondered who could help me identify exactly which wand I had in my hands, and a flash of insight crossed my mind. But of course. I could take it to my science teacher from last year, Mrs. Lambert. She knew a lot about plants. *I'm a genius!*

I immediately put the wand in my backpack so I wouldn't forget it on Monday. I'd worked enough for now and direly needed a break. Why should I be the one to stop Brianna anyway? As long as she stayed out of my life, I didn't have to worry.

My stomach was rumbling with anticipation. I still hadn't eaten, and it was noon. I came out of my den, determined to get back to my normal life. Feeling refreshed, I ate the lasagna my mother had prepared for my family.

With my stomach full, I summoned the courage to call William and sort out what had happened between us.

I went back to my room. With the door locked, I searched my contact list for William's number. Stress coursed through my veins. A ring. I didn't know exactly what to say. Two rings. Did I really still have feelings for Christian? Three rings. Christian would never be interested in me anyway. A click told me I had reached William's voice mail. I hung up and sent him a text.

Please let me explain.

I left my room and spent a normal afternoon with my family. For a time, I almost forgot about Brianna. I was playing or arguing with my little sister. I felt normal, even carefree.

I checked my phone. Still no answer from William. My heart sank painfully. Would he forgive me?

On Facebook, I was tagged in several photos from the Halloween party, including one where I was smiling and posing with Brianna. We looked great, and the world was at our feet. There were tons of positive comments about our fabulous costumes and even more likes. I felt a twinge of regret at the prospect of saying goodbye to all that.

* * *

The day started with my science class. Mr. Thompson, our super-sexy teacher, was having a hard time teaching his class. He only had eyes for Brianna, who was winking at him and giving him greedy glances. I silently ranted in my chair. Did the other students realize what was going on? I hoped with all my heart that they didn't. If rumors reached the principal's ears, Mr. Thompson could lose his job. Even worse, if the rumors reached his wife's ears...

I had to take matters into my own hands.

First, I wanted to know more about the magic wand. As long as I was on the science floor, I went looking for Ms. Lambert right after class.

I knocked timidly on the door of the science teacher's room. As expected, I found the teacher there. She was quietly having coffee with a colleague while waiting for the next class period to begin.

"Hi, Mrs. Lambert," I said. "Can I have two minutes of your time?"

"Yes, of course, Emily. How are you? Still doing well in science?"

I blushed at the compliment. She led me down the hall.

"I can't take credit," I said. "Science classes are fascinating." Since I only had a few minutes before English class, I went straight to the point. "I need your help. Can you identify this type of wood?"

I took the wand from my bag and held it out to her. She turned it over several times in her hands.

"Ceratonia siliqua," she said.

Noticing the question marks in my eyes, she smiled and continued, "I'm sorry. It's carob wood. I could be wrong, but I'm pretty sure of what I'm saying. You see the compact, grainy structure? This wood is highly prized in cabinet factories for its hardness, its reddish color, and grain. This tree grows mostly in Mediterranean regions."

I took out my diary and hurried to note the name so I could continue my research tonight on the Internet. I asked Mrs. Lambert to spell out the Latin name for me. The bell was already ringing. I was going to be late for my English class if I didn't hurry. I thanked the teacher, put the wand back in my bag, and ran off.

Then I had to deal with my problem with William. I couldn't find him anywhere during the morning break. At lunchtime, however, I knew exactly where to find him, since he always sat at the same table in the cafeteria. So I met him there. He couldn't avoid me.

With my lunch bag in hand, I made my way over to him. He greeted me coldly.

"Can I sit down?" I asked.

"Sebastian's sitting there, but he's in line at the cafeteria," William said. "You can sit down until he gets here."

He chewed his ham sandwich without looking at me.

"Look, about Friday… I know what you're thinking, but I felt nothing for Christian. It's just that Brianna…"

"Emily, I need to think about us," he interrupted. "I don't know if I'm ready for a relationship. I'm not sure I want to continue."

I was bummed. I had obviously ruined everything. There was no need to make a fool of myself any longer, in front of all his friends, no less.

"I need time," he said in conclusion.

He had finished saying what was on his mind, and I had heard enough anyway. I held back my tears as I left him behind.

With a sore soul and a tight throat, I joined the girls and Brianna in our usual spot. I ate as much of my lunch as I could, but I wasn't hungry. I threw the rest in the trash so my mother wouldn't find out I'd barely nibbled. Brianna's angelic facade made me lose my appetite even more. *It was all her fault!*

That evening, I consulted the index of the ancient book Destiny had given me. I was looking for a spell that would prevent a manipulator from doing any harm. A counterspell, to negate the effects of Brianna's spell.

I scrolled through the index and found "Love Potion, The History of Magic Applied to Art, Art Ethics." Could that section help me? I giggled to myself. No doubt about it. Brianna could use a look at this section.

I frantically turned the pages to get to the right chapter. Feverishly, I skimmed through the text, and a subheading caught my eye—"Countering Attacks." I slowed my pace and read the text carefully. In the middle of the second paragraph, I found an incantation.

What has been done can be undone. Creation and destruction are linked.

What did those words mean? Could they be effective against Brianna? Reciting this incantation seemed simple enough, too simple even to be of any use.

I repeated the sentence mentally several times to memorize it. I thought of all the people Brianna had manipulated without remorse. The spell was probably very basic and would have little impact, but it would be a start to prevent her from doing more harm. I shuddered at the thought of using a simple incantation to stop Brianna. Destiny could give me more information. I jotted down the page number so I could refer to it the next time I met with Destiny.

Because of my studies of magic, my school studies were suffering. I was falling behind on my homework and not studying hard for my tests. Deciding to make up for lost time, I set aside the book to dive into some math problems.

While looking for my textbook in my schoolbag, my hand came across the wand of… of… what exactly had Mrs. Lambert told me?

I went in search of my diary, in which I had written the information. *Of carob tree!* Forgetting about the equations, I took out my laptop to do some research on the subject and found the Wikipedia site to be a mine of knowledge.

Carob trees measure from five to seven meters in height and can exceptionally reach fifteen meters. Widely spread, they like to grow on arid slopes. People cultivate them for their fruit, the carob. The trunks are large and twisted, the bark brown and rough. Their life span can reach five hundred years.

Wow! Five hundred years. That's really old!

I wondered how old the branch that had been used to make my wand was. I read on.

The Latin name for the carob tree, Ceratonia, comes from the Greek word keratia, meaning 'little horn,' because the tree's fruit is horn shaped when ripe.

The tree looked like a tough cookie to me. Was it because of its intimidating characteristics that the tree's bark had been selected for the wands? Because according to the book *Magic Wands and Consecrations*, the species was not usually used to make wands. The more information I found out, the more questions I had. It was really frustrating.

I woke up on Tuesday morning with newfound confidence, I reread the incantation aloud a few times to make sure that it had sunk into my mind. I was determined to hold Brianna back. It wasn't very safe to reveal my intentions to harm her, but she was going too far, and I was more than tired of doing nothing.

I had barely crossed the threshold of the school's glass doors when Brianna charged at me. She was shaking with contained rage. "Come on, we need to talk!"

She grabbed my forearm with force and pulled me violently into an empty hallway. Her fingers dug into my flesh, and I could not pull away. I wondered how I could lure her away.

"You did this. Admit it!" she hissed through her teeth, pinning me to the wall.

"I don't know what you're talking about," I said, straightening my back and glaring at her. I had no intention of letting her intimidate me.

"Mr. Thompson didn't even look at me this morning, nor did the girls. It's as if I don't exist!"

"Really?" I asked in disbelief.

Who had undone Brianna's spells? Destiny? Or had it been me when I read the spell this morning? *No way!*

Her slap took me by surprise, and my head flew into the wall behind me. With the imprint of her hand on my cheek burning with pain, I turned to challenge her. Despite myself, my eyes filled with tears.

Her eyes glowed with fury. But that flicker was quickly extinguished when she saw my eyes were not fearful, but determined. She stepped back hesitantly. I said in a powerful voice that echoed through the corridor:

"What has been done can be undone. Creation and destruction are linked."

A shock wave spread through the school grounds, with me as its epicenter. The floor vibrated.

Brianna lost consciousness and fell to the ground, inert. I stood still, dumbfounded. Alarmed, a teacher-supervisor who was turning the corner rushed over to her.

"Brianna, can you hear me?" He took out his mobile phone and contacted the emergency service.

Curious people approached us. A deafening hubbub was rising from the growing crowd. Other teachers rushed over to dispel the mass of panicked and curious teenagers. Ambulance sirens sounded, growing steadily louder. Brianna was still lying on the ground, still unconscious, despite the care of the proctor.

I was motionless. Had I hurt Brianna? I didn't understand what had just happened.

"Emily, what happened?" My English teacher was leaning toward me.

I was speechless. My vision blurred. Paramedics arrived, pushed through the crowd, and rushed to Brianna's side, pulling a stretcher behind them. One of the paramedics approached me. In a haze, I heard my teacher say, "She's in shock."

The paramedic pulled me aside. He sat me down on a bench and wrapped me in a thermal blanket. I felt myself slowly coming to my senses. I noticed I was shaking uncontrollably.

"I'm fine," I said.

The paramedic leaned over to observe me. My words left him skeptical.

"How is Brianna?" I asked in a louder voice.

"We're going to take her to the hospital and put her under observation and run some tests. She should be fine. Don't worry."

Ashamed and worried, I remained silent. I knew I had not cast a minor fainting spell. Whatever I'd done had hurt Brianna. Guilt poured out of every pore of my skin. I hoped the paramedic wouldn't notice.

He took my vitals and nodded. "I'll take you back to the infirmary. Let you get over your shock in peace. You'll be back on your feet in no time."

He closed his medical bag and handed me over to the school nurse, who was approaching.

But what had I done? I had to get out of there, find a corner, and think about it.

"So, Emily, the paramedic told me you were already feeling better." The school nurse led me gently into the infirmary. She pushed open the door and pointed to a bed. "You can lie there and rest as long as you like."

"I have to go home," I said. "Can I be excused for the day?"

Her eyebrows arched in surprise. "You can't leave. You are still in shock, and you are my responsibility."

I lay down on the small bed. Several minutes later, I tried again to get permission to be dismissed.

The nurse inspected me, trying to decide if I was fit to leave. "All right. I'll call your mom, and she'll pick you up."

"No need," I said, picking up my jacket, then walked toward the door and opened it. "I'll call a cab. Thanks."

"But wait a minute!" she protested.

I let the door to the infirmary close behind me. I ran to the school exit, still a little shaky, determined not to be forced back into the infirmary.

I hurriedly hailed a taxi and got in. I wanted to go home and think about the latest events, but I gave the driver Destiny's address. I arrived at her house without having given her advance warning. After a few quick knocks on her door, I burst into her house without even waiting for an answer.

"Destiny, are you here?" I called.

She came out of her consulting room.

I rushed toward her. "Brianna, she fell. I made her fall. It's my fault!"

I was sobbing now, my shoulders shaking.

Destiny shook me firmly. "Take a deep breath, my dear, and tell me clearly what's going on." She guided me to the round table in the cramped room. "Sit here."

Fortunately, she wasn't meeting with a client.

I took a deep breath of air. "I said an incantation. In front of Brianna. One I found in the book you lent me. And she collapsed in front of me!"

She jumped to her feet and slammed her palms on the table, leaning forward. I had never seen her in such a state.

"You cast a spell from that book! I warned you! Trusting a teenager, I should've known better," she said to herself.

She began pacing the tiny room. "Which spell? What spell did you cast?"

I recited, "What has been done can—"

She interrupted me. "You mustn't recite that incantation lightly! You don't seem to have learned anything!"

I bowed my head in shame. Destiny had let me consult her books, and I had promised to use only the spells she approved. In my anger, I hadn't thought about the consequences.

"I didn't know that this spell would be so powerful." I knew it was a poor excuse, but it was all I could think of at that moment.

Destiny came back to the table to sit across from me and leaned over. "The intensity of an incantation depends on many factors. Experience, emotions, the raw power of the summoner… I could have told you about this before. I'm still bitterly disappointed."

Again, I lowered my head. I could not afford to lose Destiny's help. She was my guide and teacher. "I am so sorry. I need your help."

"Now that you've discovered your powers, it would be even more irresponsible to let you go without a balanced education and a crash course in ethics." She sighed. "Tell me what happened. Don't leave out any details."

I described the scene from the moment Brianna led me down the hall to my exit from the infirmary, without saying the magic words this time.

Destiny muttered to herself. She didn't look happy. "You just don't realize what this means. I had my doubts about the extent of your magical strength, but what you've done is beyond my expectations. With great power comes great responsibility!"

I laughed in disbelief.

"What?"

"You've been watching *Spiderman* lately," I said, laughing. "That line is straight out of that movie."

Destiny frowned.

"The fact remains that it is a great truth. Emily"—she said, taking my hands in hers—"you must be extremely careful. Witches have been in hiding since the beginning of time. Ordinary people have never accepted them. Some witches are dangerous."

A shadow passed over Destiny's face.

"There is a whole secret community of people with powers, and they will do anything to draw you to them, especially with the power you hold," she said. "Beware of them."

A shiver ran down my spine. I didn't want all that power. "Right now, all I care about is getting Brianna out of harm's way. But without hurting her."

"Let me do some research," Destiny said. "I have a better idea of what you're capable of now, so the research might come in handy."

I stood up. The conversation with Destiny was over. She was already bustling about the room, looking through her jumble of books.

I went straight home. Before I turned the handle on the front door, I took a deep breath and put on my mask of impassivity. Pretending that everything was fine in front of my family was more trying and tiring than anything else.

Chapter 9

I was anxious about returning to school the next day. What had the other students been saying while I was away? Rumors spread like wildfire at my small school.

Yet no one paid any attention to me. Strangely, everything seemed as usual. I watched the students behaving normally. No one was staring at me. No one was slandering me. Something strange and inexplicable was happening.

Inexplicable… until Brianna turned the corner, surrounded by her *best friends*. Wasn't she supposed to stay in the hospital for a few days for observation? She seemed to be in great shape.

As she passed me, she gave me a beaming smile and a delighted wink. *What arrogance!* I fumed. In a flash, I understood. She had put all her manipulation spells back in place. She was brazenly defying me. I would not let that stand. Like a child, I stamped my foot to vent my rage.

I had no intention of going to class. This reality was not the right one, and I had to restore order. I hurried home to consult the ancient book Destiny have given me. I needed an even more powerful incantation, one that Brianna would not dare counteract, one she could not thwart.

I pushed open the door to the house and found my mom, dad, and sister sitting on the couch, watching TV and stuffing themselves with chips and candy.

"What the hell are you doing here?" I asked. "Dad, shouldn't you be at work? Mom, don't you have a big meeting? And Lillian, it's pottery day at the day care. You've been talking about it all week!"

"I'd rather stay home," Lillian said. "I don't feel well."

"Neither do we," my parents replied mechanically in unison, then stuffed their faces with junk food.

I stood in front of them, speechless, then tried shaking them. There was nothing I could do. Were they maybe under the power of a manipulation spell? I ran down the stairs to my room in the basement to dive into the grimoire. I remembered learning a spell to find out if a person was being controlled. But it was in the book of spells for beginners, the book I had returned to Destiny. I hoped to find a similar spell in the ancient book.

I scanned the index at lightning speed and came upon just what I was looking for—a short incantation. Nothing could be simpler. Relieved that I didn't have to gather any strange materials, I scanned the instructions.

"Recite this incantation aloud to the person you suspect of being manipulated by a spell," I read aloud. "Look her in the eye, and you will discover the truth."

I took the book with me, holding my place with my finger, and climbed the stairs two at a time to join my family in the living room. I opened the book and blurted out the incantation.

"Let your eyes reveal what your actions betray."

My three family members looked up and stared at me. I cried out in fright.

Their eyes were completely white.

I ran out of the house, carrying the grimoire under my arm.

I heard my family giggling madly before I slammed the door behind me. It was horrifying. I couldn't bear to stay in the house another minute.

Despite the cool weather, I sat on the steps of the stoop to consult the ancient book. Brianna had nerve to attack my family. A rush of rage came over me.

"You've gone too far, old girl!" I said aloud. "I'll unleash all the demons of hell on you. Now it's personal!"

Where could I find an incantation like the one I had used on Brianna? In my frenzy, I could remember none of the words. Finally, I came across the right section of the book. *It contains the same incantation!* I returned to the living room and stood in front of my family. It was heartbreaking to see them like this, but what if the incantation went wrong and they ended up in the hospital? I swallowed hard. *Destiny would hate me!*

Lillian gave me a strange look and stuffed a handful of sweets into her mouth with a strange grunt. I had no other choice, so I read the words.

"What has been done can be undone. Creation and destruction are linked."

No reaction. Lillian and my parents continued to devour junk food and giggle. I hadn't expected that. The first time I'd tried the spell, I had put an end to manipulation spells controlling the entire school. Now I couldn't even do it on my family. I must have lacked conviction. Destiny had taught me that the intensity of the witch's feelings influenced the strength of the spell cast. I had doubted my incantation would work. My confusion had surely diminished the power of my words.

I closed my eyes, determined to give the incantation my best shot. I drew on the anger that washed over me from head to toe. Rage consumed my every cell, then I took a deep breath and pounded the air with every word.

"What has been done can be undone. Creation and destruction are linked."

I had channeled all my energy into the incantation, and yet nothing happened. It seemed as though Brianna had perfected her art as well. My spell was no longer enough to defeat hers. I bitterly regretted revealing my powers to her. Then she would have had no reason to perfect her magic, and even worse, to attack my family.

Devastated, I dropped to the living room carpet with the book open in my hands. My parents threw popcorn crumbs at me and laughed—raucous, demonic laughs. I was the one responsible for their condition, and I didn't know what to do about it.

A salty tear rolled down my cheek. My sister jumped up, wiped it away with her index finger, and brought it to her mouth. Her crazy eyes fluttered in her sockets. I couldn't stand the sight of her. It broke my heart and disgusted me at the same time.

I didn't know what to do. I had my family to save, the school to free, and finally, Brianna to get rid of permanently. I didn't know how to accomplish any of those three actions, but I had to find out. My priority right now was to undo the spell on my family.

I opened Destiny's book once more, flipped to the table of contents, and skimmed through the topics. Nothing. Again, more slowly. *Nothing!* I jumped to my feet to leave the house. I couldn't bear to see my family like this because of me. It was clouding my mind, and I needed all my concentration.

With resolve, I stuffed the two ancient books and the wand into my backpack. I rushed out the door, unable to look at my family for another second. As I crossed the threshold, I heard an ominous gurgle from my mother's throat. I swallowed hard as I closed the door behind me.

Once outside, the cool breeze lifted my hair. Although it was already November, the temperature was strangely pleasant. The timid sun was warming the earth as best as it could. I took a deep breath of fresh air. I was not thinking clearly. Where to go now? What to do?

I did not realize that my steps had led me to the cemetery. I found a worn tombstone and leaned against it. The ground was cold. I had to get Brianna out of our lives once and for all.

Ominous clouds were gathering in the sky, hiding the sun.

Suddenly, I heard a chuckle, and a chill ran down my spine. I turned and saw Brianna coming toward me through the tombstones.

"I was looking for you, my friend," she said.

I leapt to my feet to confront her. Brianna didn't seem to notice my disgust and rage, or she consciously ignored it. She approached with her characteristic catlike steps, exuding confidence.

"I want to offer you the chance to form an alliance," Brianna said. "We could combine our powers and get the lives we want. Anything we want!"

"What about my family? Why did you have to bring them into this?"

She laughed contemptuously. "I just wanted to get your attention. Don't worry. If you accept my proposal, I'll cancel the spell."

She obviously expected a reaction from me. When she didn't see any change in my expression, she continued, "Don't you love this new life I've created for us? Isn't this what you wanted most in the world? You were bored to death before I came to this rotten village."

I clenched my fists. She was circling me, listing the advantages of a partnership with her. "You can have popularity, admiration, and the easy life of someone for whom everything is taken for granted. All you have to do is take my hand."

She reached out her hand.

"Take my hand and take everything!"

That hand abruptly became very attractive. If I grasped it, my family would be safe, I could have fun, and I could have everything I wanted. Why not team up with Brianna, after all?

Because she's evil!

And Destiny had warned me not to use magic to my advantage, that a witch's soul grew darker and darker with each evil incantation she recited. I was convinced that I should use my powers for good, not evil. I didn't want to be like Brianna.

"No way!" I said. "You don't know the difference between right and wrong. I don't want to become a black witch!"

A frightening grin contorted her face. The shadows cast by the gravestones in the cemetery danced across her face. A fine drizzle fell.

"Emily, you understand absolutely nothing about life. Nothing!" she said contemptuously.

"Brianna, please! Come to your senses. You can't keep manipulating people like this."

She spat on the ground and straightened to her full height, looking proud. "This power is my gift. I must honor it by using it."

"You're using it wrong," I said. "Let me introduce you to my mentor. She will teach you to use your magic better, to stop doing evil."

Brianna laughed sinisterly and came closer to me, appearing threatening.

"You poor thing," she said. "I don't care about your righteous view of the world. Life is too short, and I'm going to make the most of it in my own way. I offered you a chance to join me and live this wonderful life. Yet you refuse it. Now get out of my way forever!"

She pushed me violently. I lost my balance and fell backward hard. The ground was wet under my jeans.

She smiled at me. "You belong here now, with the worms."

I stood up and rubbed my sore buttocks, brushing my jeans to get rid of the mud and grass. The drizzle turned into freezing rain. Brianna's green eyes sparkled with rage. More than the downpour, she gave me the chills.

"Stay out of my way!" she cried. "What I did to your parents was just a warning. The spell will end on its own after twenty-four hours."

She was hovering around me. I couldn't take my eyes off her. She was completely crazy. Her hair was dripping wet, the same as mine.

"If you even once try to get in my way, I will go after your family in a much more perverse and, unfortunately for you, permanent way," she warned.

I felt anger roar within me.

"So, we understand each other?" she asked.

I was boiling with rage. My fists clenched. I certainly would not let her take out her anger at me on my family. Brianna took my silence as consent.

"It was a pleasure to do business with you," she said in a deceptively courteous tone. She bowed and winked at me. That was the last straw. She turned away, ready to leave the cemetery.

I'm not letting her get away with this!

"Just a moment, Brianna," I said.

She stopped dead in her tracks.

"I don't accept your proposal, and I have no intention of letting you hurt my family."

She turned and glared at me. I caught up with her and faced her. The rain was coming down harder, but I was not cold. The anger that burned inside me warmed me.

"You got it, little bitch!" I said, enraged. "Every spell you cast, I'll be there, behind you, and I'll undo them, one by one, even if it takes my life!"

To my surprise, Brianna seemed delighted that I was confronting her. She clapped sarcastically.

"Bravo, Emily," she said. "I was hoping in my heart that you would give me the opportunity to eliminate you. I expected this reaction from you."

She clasped her hands together, the right one on top of the left, then gradually moved them apart. A ball of red energy formed and grew in her hands, and I felt my eyes grow wide. The ball of energy crackled dangerously. But how did it—

The ball came toward me, and I threw myself facedown on the ground to avoid it. A scorching smell reached my nostrils. The ball had fried a few strands of my hair. It was attacking me. Did it want to kill me? Suddenly, fear paralyzed me. I did not want to fight to the death. I just wanted to practice good values, and now I was facing death.

I felt a rush of adrenaline run through my body. Pressing my palms into the mud, I turned just in time to see a second ball of light hurtling toward me. I rolled to the side to avoid it.

"Brianna! You've completely lost your mind!" I said in a

panic.

I needed to think fast. How could I defend myself? My hand slipped into my bag and closed on Brianna's wand. I pulled it out and pointed it at her. Brianna looked surprised then laughed.

"No one knows how to use wands anymore, so don't think you can scare me with that twig," she said. "I'm more powerful than you."

Indeed, no matter how hard I concentrated and waved the wand, nothing happened.

Exasperated by my behavior, she threw another ball at me with even more force. This time I could not avoid it, and excruciating pain shot up my left arm. The wand slipped from my hand and flew, landing on a tombstone.

I cringed in pain. Brianna obviously had no intention of sparing me. She ignored my pleas and continued to attack me. I dodged her electric balls as best I could, but Brianna was getting dangerously close to me.

Quick, Emily. Think!

Brianna's strength seemed to be running out. *Eureka!* Producing those balls of light must have taken a lot of energy and drained her magic. She had already thrown several of them at me. They were getting smaller now, and it was taking her longer to form them. I took advantage of the moment of respite to get up and run away.

"You won't get away that easily!" Brianna called.

She chased after me, caught up to me, and slammed me hard to the ground. I turned and tried to hit her, but she grabbed my wrists and pinned me down. She crushed me with all her weight, and I felt like I was suffocating. I was angry at myself for not having put more heart into my physical education classes.

I was weak and helpless because of my failing.

I squirmed under Brianna, and the mud splashed all over us. It was in my mouth. My soggy hair was sticking to my face. My only advantage was that Brianna had been weakened by her use of magic.

I changed my strategy. I slowed my movements to give her the impression that I was too weak to resist anymore. Then I gathered all the strength I had left to quickly roll to the side and throw Brianna to the ground. I was now in control. I was sitting on her. She tried to punch me, but I grabbed her wrists and held her down. Enraged, Brianna let out a horrible scream.

"You bitch! You do not know the extent of my power!"

She muttered incantations at a rapid rate. I couldn't even make out the words flying out of her mouth. What was she going to do to me? How could I get rid of her once and for all? I had to silence her quickly so I wouldn't be hit by her evil spell.

An indescribable rage rose in me. I had had enough and there was no way I was going to let her do this.

I slapped her in the face, and the sound echoed throughout the cemetery. Brianna's head snapped back. Surprised, she stared at me for a moment. At least she'd stopped saying her evil words. We were both dazed by my action. I could see her cheek turning red. Coming to, eyes wide with anger, Brianna screamed at me.

"You just made your last mistake!" she said, projecting herself toward me.

She threw me off my feet, and I lost my balance. I landed hard in the mud, hitting my head. Brianna was on top of me, her hands around my neck. She uttered her incantation again, even faster and louder. She was clearly putting all her conviction into it, and I felt that whatever she was doing to me would have terrible consequences. Her crazy, bloodshot eyes bulged out.

I was so scared. Was I going to see my family again?

I felt bad. Terrible. Despite the cold, a warmth invaded me from within like a whirlwind. I was running out of air. Brianna still squeezed my neck. Overwhelmed by the fire boiling inside me, I writhed in pain on the muddy grass.

Suddenly, Brianna's voice changed dramatically and faded away. Her cruel smile vanished abruptly. Her hands released my throat. In shock, I coughed loudly, trying to catch my breath. To my relief, the burning inside quickly faded. Why had Brianna stopped? I had thought my last hour had come. Relieved, I rolled onto my side to breathe easier. After a few minutes, I leaned on my arms and stood up, ready to run away.

But then I saw Brianna.

She was kneeling, with strands of hair stuck to her face. She was looking in all directions in apparent panic. Intrigued by her strange behavior, I turned around to find out what she was seeing.

I thought I saw menacing shadows approaching us. Five of them. Soon, the shadows turned into tall figures in long, black robes and hoods on their heads. Their faces weren't visible. A shiver ran down my spine. The way they moved gracefully, as if they were floating…

I did not know who these characters were, but I would rather never find out. Nothing about them reassured me. Brianna's reaction only amplified my distrust of the newcomers.

Brianna stood up and brought her hands up with her palms facing outward, as if she were in front of the police. She seemed to be pleading with the shadowy figures and showing her submission. I followed her lead, and my whole body protested, sending shocks of pain through me. That fight had exhausted me.

If I get out of this alive, I swear I'm going to go to the gym and get in serious shape.

The sinister shadows surrounded us, forming a circle. There was no way out. I glanced at Brianna. Were we going to join forces to deal with this new threat? One of the shadowy figures raised its hands, pulled off its hood, and revealed its face.

Although the rain was dripping on her features, I could see that the face was that of an exquisite woman. Her waterproof mascara highlighted her iridescent pale-brown eyes. She turned to Brianna.

"Brianna, you know what you're in for," she said simply.

The woman's face was impassive. Brianna's expression crumbled. I couldn't understand it.

"We don't give third chances," the woman said. "We warned you three years ago in Denmark. Then a year ago in Mexico. Now we're meeting again."

Grunts of assent went up from the others in the circle. A new shiver of horror shook me.

"Wait, you don't understand!" Brianna cried in a panicked voice. "Emily, explain it to them."

It was easy to read the fear on her face.

"I understand nothing," I said. "What do you want me to tell them? What have you done now, Brianna? Who are these people?"

The woman turned and looked—or rather, stared—at me for the first time.

"You're a witch too. Are you affiliated with this one?" she asked, pointing at Brianna.

"She was my best friend," I said. "But I don't agree with her decisions. She brings evil to everyone around her. And she put a spell on my family!"

"Shh!" Brianna said and glared at me.

I didn't like to rat anyone out, but it was all I could do at the moment. Maybe these shadowy figures would help me stop Brianna and prevent her from doing any more harm.

"It was only a temporary spell, your grace. I had no intention of hurting them," Brianna said submissively. She twisted her hands nervously and scanned the ground. She looked harmless. *What an actress!*

"Enough of this!"

The sound of the woman's threatening voice bounced off the tombstones and echoed in my skull. Even the rain seemed afraid of her command and stopped falling at that very moment. *Finally.*

I was still soaked to the bone and covered in mud. I was shivering.

"You leave us no choice now," the woman said. "We have to enforce the code."

"No!" cried Brianna.

Brianna ran like a frantic gazelle, desperately seeking a gap between the figures. The circle closed in on us.

The woman turned her exquisite face to me. "It's time for you to go."

Hands appeared from under a toga. Another woman, whose face I could not make out, grabbed me and quickly threw me out of the circle. Brianna was alone to face the shadowy figures, who could only be witches. I ran for cover a little farther away. I hid behind a tombstone that had an angel carved on top, as if to watch the scene. What would the witches do to her?

"I beg of you! I have learned my lesson! I won't do it again!" Brianna cried, curled up on the damp ground.

"There's no point in arguing. You had your chance, and you didn't take it," the beautiful woman said, replacing her hood.

Brianna was crying now. She was swaying back and forth, as if she had gone mad. The witches gathered around her, arm in arm.

"Let us begin!" the woman said.

An intense murmur arose. The five witches were saying an incantation in unison. They began softly, then their litany became more and more forceful. They repeated the same words over and over.

"Nigrum pythonissam es fundati. Da tuis magicis in natura."

Intrigued, I watched everything from my hiding place, even though the head witch had ordered me to leave.

A delicate blue powder rose from Brianna's small, curled body. What were they doing to her? Were they going to kill her?

More and more powder was rising, creating a thick, swirling cloud above and around them. I could hardly make out the figures now through the fog.

Then the lyrics changed.

"Veniat ad me. Veniat ad me."

The blue cloud grew in size and formed a beautiful swirl. I was breathless. Brianna sobbed weakly. At least she was still alive.

The cloud split into five parts under the influence of the words spoken by the five witches. In perfect synchronization, they sucked in the blue cloud through their mouths.

I watched in awe as they soaked up the shiny powder. I was speechless at the dazzling and disturbing sight. The witches had almost finished swallowing everything by now.

Some blue residue continued to float in the air despite the

insistence of the shadowy figures who continued to suck in the powder. The spell did not seem to be following its expected course.

Anxiety washed over me. Was my presence causing the problem? Had the witches discovered my hiding place? I choked with fear and let out a gurgle. Worried that the noise had alerted them, I held my breath.

In a blinding flash of blue, the rest of the dust rushed into my mouth. With violence, it forced its way into my lungs. I choked. It disgusted me that I had ingested a substance from Brianna's body. Was I going to get cancer?

Of course, the witches spotted me immediately. They broke the circle, leaving Brianna trembling on the ground. She looked defeated and lethargic. She was still crying, curled up in the mud with her head on her lap. The witches must have finished with Brianna, and now they were interested in me. They wanted to absorb my blue powder. I was shaking more and more.

The head witch came toward me. She uncovered her face. "You should have run away when I told you."

Was she going to torture me? Extract my soul? It sounded absolutely terrifying.

"But nature chose you," she said. "Today, she gave you the gift of even more power."

She looked pensive.

"We will meet again," she said, replacing her black hood.

She walked away with the other witches. It was all over. I was safe, and so was Brianna.

I ran to her and gently patted her back to comfort her.

"Brianna, they're gone," I said "Don't worry. Everything's fine."

My words of encouragement seemed to bring her back to life. She suddenly stood up, shoving me aside. "You understand nothing, you stupid bitch! They took my magic. They stole it from me! I'm nothing now."

Fat tears streamed down her face. She ran out of the cemetery.

With my adrenaline rush over, an indescribable heaviness assailed all my limbs and my mind. Through the fog, one thought arose.

Go home.

My survival instinct drove me to my feet. I retrieved Destiny's soaked books from the frozen mud and found the wand, which I held on to despite its apparent uselessness. Then I dragged myself back to my house.

I pushed open the door to my house. Strangely, everything was quiet. I saw neither my parents nor my sister. Despite the dirt on my clothes, I collapsed on the sofa and fell asleep immediately.

Chapter 10

I did not wake until the next morning. My skin was covered with bruises, and my back ached from sleeping so long on the couch.

Suddenly, I remembered the day before. Where was my family?

I got up in a hurry to look around the house. I went to Lillian's room. She was fast asleep, with a blond strand of hair in her face and her favorite teddy bear in her arms. Even though she was tangled up in her sheets, she looked like an angel. She had always been a fitful sleeper. I gently tucked a lock of hair behind her ear.

Soothed, I rushed to my parents' room and knocked three times on the door.

"Come in," my mother said, just loudly enough for me to hear.

My father was still asleep beside her in the bed. His steady breathing sounded like a boat motor, which always made my sister and me laugh. I walked over to the bed.

"You're a late sleeper this morning," I said to my mother.

"I don't know why, but I feel completely drained," she said. "I called the office to say I was ill and your father too. Until Lillian is up and about, I'm staying in bed."

My family was back to normal. I was so happy to see my mother again, I put my arms around her neck and breathed a sigh of relief.

"And you? How are you? Why are you so dirty?" she asked, suddenly worried.

I examined my outfit in the light of day. I needed a good shower, and my jeans would go straight into the garbage. Too bad. They looked good on me.

"You'll have to explain to me what happened," my mother said. "I feel strange this morning, and now I have a headache."

"Can I take time off too?" I also felt exhausted. "I've already missed my first two classes anyway."

"I'll call the school to explain your absence," she said. "Don't worry. Today can be a family day."

"Great," I said, in a good mood despite my aching muscles. "This morning, I'm making breakfast."

I stomped out of the room. I whistled and mixed the pancake mixture. When Lillian got up, she jumped into my arms. I ruffled her hair.

"Great. Pancakes!" Lillian cried.

"There is something for everyone," I said.

"I want maple syrup and blueberries on mine!" Lillian was jumping around the island. The butter was crackling in the pan, and I was pouring the batter. My mother and father came into the kitchen, stretching. They had put on their dressing gowns.

"It smells good in here," my father said.

I stayed home from school on Thursday, surrounded by my family. On Friday, everyone took another day off work and school. I had a long weekend to rest and spend time with my family. I had been so afraid for their safety.

The following Monday, I was eager to get back to school and to run into Brianna. Would my friends ask me why I had been absent last Thursday and Friday? I didn't know what excuse to make up to hide my clandestine life as a witch's apprentice.

I opened the big, glass door and walked over to our table. As usual, Ashley, Caroline, Joe, Morgan, and Vanessa were there. They were chatting. Everything seemed so normal. Couldn't they see that the world had just turned upside down?

Brianna wasn't present.

"Hello, Emily." Ashley greeted me when I sat down next to her. "Have you recovered?"

"What?" I asked. "What are you talking about?"

Had she heard about my adventure in the cemetery?

"Well, you were sick, weren't you?" Ashley said.

Phew! "I feel better today," I said.

"Have you seen Brianna today? I heard she moved," Ashley said, looking relieved.

"No, I haven't seen her." If Brianna had moved, I was even more thankful than Ashley was. Finally, gossip I was happy to hear. I wanted to know all the details. "What else have you heard?"

"She's been missing since Thursday," Ashley said. "She wasn't in class, and nobody knows where she is. I heard two teachers talking about her in the hallway on Friday. They said she and her aunt moved away! Just like that."

She snapped her fingers.

"Gone, as if by magic!" she added.

I was pretty sure she didn't mean it literally.

The girls all agreed that it was best not to have Brianna around. They seemed to expect me to contradict them, but I did not. Brianna's hasty departure was the best thing that could have happened to me.

Everything went back to normal at the little high school in Frankville. I never thought I would say this, but I was thrilled about it. After so much chaos, I found happiness in the smallest things. I was learning to appreciate my friends, whom I had known all my life, in a new light. They had always been there for me even though we didn't have that much in common.

I might as well make the most of these last moments before leaving for college.

The winter holidays were fast approaching, so I focused on my studies to prepare for my final exams and forgot about Brianna and magic. I would soon enjoy a few weeks off to rest with my family. *I can't wait!*

The last day of school finally ended. When I came home, I found a small cardboard box on the doorstep. My name was written in neat cursive on it. I picked up the box and shook it gently. Objects moved around inside. It was heavy.

I rushed to my room and opened it. I found an assortment of intriguing things, which I examined one by one—books, amulets, plants, and several odds and ends that were undoubtedly related to magic. A letter was folded at the very bottom of the box. I unfolded it and saw that it was from Destiny.

Dear Emily,

I heard that Brianna and her aunt left town. I guess they couldn't stand the humiliation of Brianna being stripped of all her powers by the Circle.

With shame, I realized I hadn't called Destiny since Brianna's departure or even brought her books back. I should have at least told her what had happened and especially thanked her for all the help she'd given me. I had immersed myself in my studies, forgetting everything else. Embarrassed, I continued reading.

I imagine that now that it no longer disrupts your life, you may not wish to continue your initiation into this universe. I am sending you some trinkets that may well pique your curiosity and make you want to discover more. There is great power within you, and I can help you unleash it. You could have a life full of adventure!

Don't forget that I will be here if you decide to pursue your destiny.
Your friend,
Destiny LaGrande

I folded the letter. The Christmas holidays were starting. I was exhausted from all the hours of studying, and I was dreaming of savoring the delicious holiday feasts concocted by my relatives. For now, I just wanted to enjoy the moment.

Why grow my magical powers? I don't need them to be happy!

I closed the lid of the box over its contents and put it on the top shelf in my closet.

A picture of Brianna and me, both of us beaming, slid across the floor. Her eyes sparkled with intelligence, and her beautiful cascade of red hair shone.

I grabbed the photo, crumpled it into a little ball, and threw it into the wastebasket.

Despite myself, a shiver of fear ran down my spine at the thought that Brianna was lurking somewhere in the shadows, hoping to steal her powers back.

About the Author

I love to provide value and entertainment to readers. That's why I write in different genres: non-fiction, science fiction, and fantasy.

I am Canadian and have lived in Mexico and the United States.

I thank you for purchasing this book. It is a pleasure for my to tell stories and your purchase encourages me to continue my creative work.

Let's keep in touch!

You can connect with me on:
- http://josianefortin.ca/en/writer
- https://ko-fi.com/jfortin

Subscribe to my newsletter:
- http://eepurl.com/hd-AQn